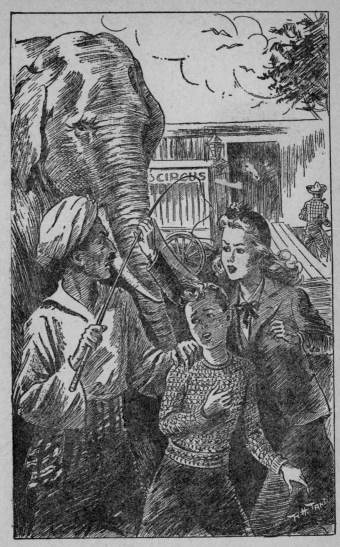

"DON'T DARE TO STRIKE THAT BOY AGAIN!"
NANCY COMMANDED.

The Mystery of the Ivory Charm

NANCY DREW MYSTERY STORIES

THE MYSTERY OF
THE IVORY CHARM

BY

CAROLYN KEENE

AUTHOR OF THE SECRET OF THE OLD CLOCK,
THE CLUE IN THE DIARY,
THE MESSAGE IN THE HOLLOW OAK, ETC.

This book, while produced under
wartime conditions, in full com-
pliance with government regula-
tions for the conservation of paper
and other essential materials, is
COMPLETE AND UNABRIDGED

NEW YORK
GROSSET & DUNLAP
PUBLISHERS

Made in the United States of America

CONTENTS

iii

iv   Contents

THE MYSTERY OF
THE IVORY CHARM

CHAPTER I

FORTUNE TELLING

NANCY DREW, neatly dressed in a blue traveling suit, her golden hair bound snugly beneath a modish little hat, sighed as she addressed her companions, the Fayne and Marvin girls, who stood beside her on the station platform.

"This certainly isn't the most pleasant way to end a delightful vacation," she commented.

"We've been waiting only an hour, but it seems an eternity," returned one of her chums, who was not only boyish looking, but was always called George Fayne. She stared down the long expanse of gleaming track. "It's my private opinion that all trains have been discontinued on this poky old line," she added.

"Are you really so eager to return to River Heights, Nancy?" Bess Marvin inquired curiously.

"I'm sorry the vacation has ended, but in a way I'll be glad to get home. One can't play all the time."

For the past month the three friends had spent a happy, care-free vacation at a camp in the mountains. They had enjoyed hiking, swimming, horseback riding and mountain climbing; the outdoor life had brought a becoming color to their cheeks. Yet during the final week, Nancy had found the steady routine of fun slightly monotonous, and she was not especially sorry to be returning home.

"I think Nancy secretly was disappointed because she failed to unearth a mystery at camp," George said teasingly.

"The mystery I'd like to solve right now is that of our train!"

"Girls! I do believe it's coming!" Bess exclaimed joyfully. "The block signal just dropped."

The three chums were gathering together their luggage when the station agent emerged from the depot, a train order in his hand.

"Number 6 is reported another half hour late," he told them with a regretful smile. "This one coming is a special freight."

In deep disgust the girls sat down on their suitcases again and with scant interest watched the approach of the train. It thundered into the station and the engineer began switching off several cars to an adjoining siding.

"Circus cars!" Nancy exclaimed, her interest quickening.

"A circus would come to town just as we're leaving," George commented in disappointment.

"Well, at least we can watch the unloading of the animals," Nancy said. "Come on, let's cross over to the siding. Our train won't arrive for at least half an hour."

Welcoming any diversion which would help to pass the time, the girls established themselves in the vicinity of the circus cars. The unloading went forward with routine precision. Attendants shouted orders as they dragged forth boxes of equipment and various canvas-covered cages of snarling, wild animals.

"I wish we could see what's inside," George complained.

"At least they can't box up the elephant," Nancy chuckled. "They're unloading him now farther down the track."

The girls drew close to watch as the huge jungle animal was induced to emerge from the car. He was coaxed and guided by a handsome little brown boy of not more than twelve years of age. The lad kept the ponderous elephant under astonishing control. Now and then he uttered a sharp command in a language which the girls did not understand.

"It's marvelous the way that lad handles the elephant!" Nancy commented in awe. "He

scarcely uses the hook at all. He seems to control him through the animal's affection for him!''

''They make an interesting pair,'' Bess remarked. ''The boy so small and the elephant so huge.''

''The lad must be from India,'' Nancy mused.

While the girls watched and marveled at the small attendant's skill, a dark-skinned man of middle age, dressed in a white uniform with gold braid and wearing a cumbersome turban on his head, came running along the tracks toward the bull car. His face became convulsed with anger as he bore down upon the Indian lad.

''You Coya!'' he shouted furiously. ''Always you pay no heed to the words of Rai! You are too lazy and worthless to use the hook!''

''But Rai, I do not require it,'' the lad protested in a musical, sing-song voice. ''Old Tom obeys my every command. Watch, I will show you.''

''It is Rai who will show you instead!'' the man cried furiously. ''I will teach you!''

Seizing the boy by the arm he began to beat him cruelly with a small jeweled whip. The terrified lad uttered a cry of fear and pain which caused the elephant to swing its trunk nervously and to emit a protesting scream.

For a moment the girls feared that the animal meant to turn upon the attacker.

"Oh! Oh!" Bess murmured, covering her eyes.

It was Nancy who sprang forward to assist the lad from India. Without stopping to consider the possible consequence of her act, she jerked the whip from the man's hand.

"Don't dare to strike that boy again!" she commanded. "He has done nothing to deserve punishment."

The man turned glaring eyes upon her. "My son is lazy," he said in haughty, clipped English. "It is my right and duty to whip him."

"But the boy was doing his work splendidly. You have no sympathy for his method of handling the elephant because it differs from yours. Please don't whip him again."

The man shrugged and abruptly turned his back upon Nancy. To Coya he said harshly:

"Rai will show you how to handle an elephant."

Grasping the hook he dug it sharply into the animal's neck, uttering a loud, terse command. The elephant did not move. Enraged, Rai repeated the move, using the instrument with cruel force.

"Oh, Rai!" the boy protested in distress.

The man tried again without success to force the elephant to obey, and then, as Coya pleaded with him to give up the hook, tossed it angrily

on the ground and walked away. Left alone, the lad spoke gently to Old Tom and with a light, guiding tap, caused the animal to move off obediently.

Nancy and her chums retreated to the shade of a nearby tree, for the noonday sun shone down with blinding intensity. They were discussing the scene which they had just witnessed, when George caught a glimpse of Rai coming toward them.

"It looks as if you're in for trouble, Nancy."

However, when Rai approached the girls his face was drawn into a grimace evidently intended for a smile. His purpose in accosting them obviously was to explain his recent behavior.

"I did not wish you to misunderstand," he said with an oily smirk. "I love Coya very dearly, but he is a lazy lad and will not work unless I use the whip."

The girls remained silent and Rai went on in a voice of forced cordiality:

"Perhaps the young ladies would be amused to have their fortunes told? Rai is said to have the ability to read the future."

Nancy was about to refuse the offer, but Bess forestalled her by saying eagerly:

"Shall we, girls? It might be fun."

"First," said Rai significantly, "my hand must be crossed with silver."

Bess found a coin in her purse which she

dropped into the native's palm. He frowned slightly as if it were not large enough, but the expression was gone in an instant and he told her a very acceptable fortune which included a year of good luck, an important letter to arrive soon, and a pleasant journey to be made in the immediate future.

"Since we're all waiting for a train now, the journey is fairly well assured," Nancy smiled.

George's turn came next and she too received a prophecy of many good things awaiting her in the coming years. It too was a routine fortune, and for that reason disappointing.

"Never mind telling mine," Nancy remarked indifferently.

Casually she leaned against a large crate which workmen had unloaded a few minutes before from the circus train and deposited near the tree. George caught her by the hand, jerking her away.

"Nancy, don't sit on that box! Can't you read the sign?"

"'Snakes!'" the Drew girl exclaimed, for the first time noticing the marking on the crate. "I'd prefer a case of dynamite!"

With a tiny shiver she started to move away, but George and Bess caught her by the hand, pulling her back to the tree where Rai stood.

"Don't be so stubborn, Nancy," Bess laughed. "Be a good girl and have your

fortune told. Then we'll all go back to the station.''

To satisfy her companions, Nancy obediently submitted herself to Rai's strange scrutiny. As he fixed his piercing dark eyes upon her face she experienced an uncomfortable sensation which she was at a loss to explain. For some moments he stared at the girl without speaking. Then, in a low, tense voice he said:

''Rai can see no good fortune ahead. Alas, my daughter, it is written that you shall have great trouble. Ay! There will be dangers to face—one which may claim your life——''

The monotonous voice of the man from India ended in a choked gasp, while Bess and George suddenly uttered a terrified scream. From the lower branches of the tree a huge jungle snake had dropped directly upon the unsuspecting Nancy, wrapping its powerful coils about her in a venomous grip of death!

CHAPTER II

An Ivory Charm

The Drew girl, temporarily paralyzed with fear, uttered no sound as the huge snake, which had escaped from a nearby circus box to take refuge in the tree, wound itself about her body. Then, recovering slightly from the shock, she made a desperate though futile effort to free herself from its tightening coils.

George and Bess, horrified at the sight, looked frantically about for weapons with which to fight off the reptile, all the while pleading with Rai to go to the aid of their chum.

The Indian's eyes bulged with superstitious fear. Instead of hurrying to Nancy's assistance he dropped down upon his knees in a state of half-trance, and in a sing-song voice began an incantation in his native tongue.

"Stop that chanting and help us!" Bess cried in distress, striking as hard as she could at the snake with a sharp stick.

George looked desperately up and down the track, shouting for assistance. Little Coya, hearing her voice, came on a run to learn what

was wrong. At one glance he took in the situation and darted away again.

George and Bess feared that the boy had been terrified at sight of the snake, but a moment later he returned with an older man. The latter, Harold Blunt, who handled the reptiles for the circus, knew exactly what to do. With Coya's assistance he quickly freed Nancy and boxed up the dangerous reptile.

Nancy's nerves were so shattered from the ordeal that with a little gasp she sank down on the grass. Her face was quite white, but she laughed shakily as Bess and George rushed to her side.

"Are you badly hurt?" Bess inquired anxiously.

"I'm not hurt at all. Only frightened. It really was nothing."

"Nothing!" George cried. "Why, it's a wonder you're alive, and you call it nothing!"

"I only meant that I'm quite all right now. I know I owe my safety to Coya."

She looked about for the Indian lad.

"He disappeared very quickly," she said with regret. "I wanted to thank him."

Harold Blunt, who had finished crating up the snake, came over to talk with Nancy and make certain that she had not been injured. Secretly he was alarmed for fear that she might intend to sue the circus for alleged damages, and was greatly relieved at the matter-

of-fact way in which she regarded the incident.

"I can't tell you how sorry I am that you were subjected to such an ordeal," he said sincerely. "The snake is not fully grown and I doubt that he could have injured you seriously. Still, the shock must have been great."

"I was a little startled when the reptile dropped down out of the tree," Nancy smiled. "It seemed as if Rai's dreadful prediction about my future might come true!"

At mention of the Indian's name attention was directed toward his kneeling figure. Although the danger was past, he continued to mutter and chant and make strange motions with his arms.

"Snap out of it, Rai!" Harold Blunt called sharply. "The snake won't get you now!"

Slowly the fortune teller arose and came toward the little group.

"A reptile will kill with a look of the eye," he muttered. "So it has been written and so it is."

"Nonsense!" Harold Blunt interrupted impatiently. "I've taken care of snakes all my life and such talk is sheer superstition."

Rai did not appear to hear this remark. His dark eyes fastened upon Nancy with an expression of awe and worship.

"You have supernatural powers," he said in a hoarse whisper. "It was that power which saved you from the reptile."

"It was the snake's owner who saved me," the girl corrected.

She turned impatiently away from Rai, but he plucked at her sleeve.

"Wait! I shall bestow upon you a gift—a wonderful charm. By so doing my own fortune will improve. So it is written."

The mention of a charm whetted Nancy's curiosity, and although the entire scene had grown distasteful to her, she could not resist waiting to learn the nature of the promised gift.

From a black velvet cord about his neck Rai withdrew a small white object. He held it for a moment in his closed fist, muttering a few unintelligible words. Then solemnly he offered it to Nancy.

She stared down at the little token. A tiny carved elephant in pure ivory! She did not make the mistake of believing that it was a cheap, crudely made trinket. Rai, in the superstitious belief that she was endowed with remarkable powers, had given her one of his choice possessions. It was a very old piece, an odd charm which hinted of a mysterious past.

Nancy's blue eyes sparkled with interest as she slowly turned the tiny elephant in her hand. How she loved mystery!

The girl had never considered herself as an amateur detective, yet in a way such a role had been forced upon her. Her first "case" had

developed when her father, Carson Drew, a famous criminal lawyer, had been too busy to investigate the strange actions of the Topham family. Nancy took up the matter herself, and in the initial volume of this group of stories, entitled "The Secret of the Old Clock," the reader learns of the clever girl's first experience in the field of mystery.

By nature Nancy was courageous and resourceful. Left motherless at an early age, she had developed an amazing ability to fight her own battles in the world. Hannah Gruen, the family housekeeper, declared that her young mistress's love of mystery would surely prove her undoing in the end, but the girl had demonstrated more than once that she had a natural aptitude for detective work.

A queer bungalow, a rambling old ranch and a mysterious inn provided background for Nancy's sleuthing abilities. Her most recent adventure, related in the volume "The Message in the Hollow Oak," carried the girl to the Canadian woods. There, while trying to protect her property, she encountered several strange characters, persons determined to steal her land and bring misfortune upon her friends.

Bess and George, who were cousins, lived in the same neighborhood at River Heights. They were proud to have shared in their chum's Canadian adventure. Now as they noticed

Nancy's excitement upon viewing the ivory charm, they suspected that she was deeply intrigued by its suggested mystery.

"The token is beautiful, Rai," Nancy murmured in awe. "But I fear it is too expensive a piece for me to keep."

"No, it is for you," the man from India insisted. "It is my wish that you wear it."

"Tell me, has the charm any particular story or significance, Rai?"

The man smiled mysteriously.

"It has a story which fades far back into the past—a strange tale of a little known, mystic province of India. This charm was once a prized possession of a great ruler—a Maharajah who is said to have been endowed with supernatural powers."

"And if I wear the charm, will these powers pass to me?" Nancy asked jokingly.

The strange man replied soberly. "The charm will so endow you. And since I have bestowed the gift upon you, my own fortune should change for the better."

"I scarcely know what to say——"

"I advise you to make up your mind quickly, Nancy!" George interrupted. "Our train is coming!"

"I'll keep the charm," the Drew girl decided instantly. "Thank you for it, Rai."

Bess and George were running toward the railway station. With the carved elephant

clutched tightly in her hand, Nancy darted after them. The girls gathered up their luggage and boarded a coach only a few seconds before it pulled out from the station.

"Imagine nearly losing our train after waiting for it all this time!" Bess gasped, as she dropped into the first available seat.

Nancy was peering from the window.

"I wish I could have talked with Coya before we left, girls. He disappeared so quickly that I didn't have an opportunity to thank him for what he did."

"He was an interesting little fellow—so bright and alert," Bess added. "It seems a shame that he has such a cruel father."

"I was amazed when Rai called Coya his son," Nancy admitted, settling herself comfortably for the ride to River Heights. "Somehow Coya seems of much finer quality."

"Well, at least Rai did you one good turn," George laughed. "Even if he didn't save you from the snake, he gave you an interesting gift."

Nancy nodded and offered the ivory charm for her chums' inspection. Now that the girls had ample time to look at the carved elephant, they were even more impressed with its workmanship.

"You're the luckiest creature I've ever known, Nancy!" Bess sighed enviously.

"I earned the charm, I think. Having a

snake drop down and give one a playful squeeze isn't exactly my idea of hilarious fun!''

"Nor mine," Bess agreed. "No, you're welcome to the gift. I don't crave it in the least."

"It may bring you bad luck instead of good, Nancy," George commented thoughtfully. "Do you really intend to wear it?"

"I haven't thought much about it yet. Of course I don't believe all that nonsense Rai was telling us."

"Not even about the mystical ruler?" Bess inquired.

"That part might be true. I haven't any faith that this charm will endow me with supernatural powers."

"I hope not," George chuckled. "You're efficient enough now!"

The girls were still discussing the bit of ivory when the conductor came through the car to collect tickets. He chatted for a moment with Nancy and her friends as he noted their destination, then passed along the aisle.

Presently, hearing a commotion at the rear of the car, the girls looked back to see what was wrong. The conductor was engaged in dragging forth a protesting boy who had hidden beneath one of the seats at the very end of the coach.

"Someone seems to be trying to steal a ride!" George observed.

Then the three girls gasped in amazement for they recognized the culprit as Coya, the Indian lad.

"You can't ride without a ticket!" the conductor told him angrily. "Either pay or off you go!"

"I can't pay," the boy answered in a frightened voice. "I have no money."

"Then off you go!"

Nancy had arisen from her seat at the front of the car. Coya's eyes fastened upon her and a hopeful light flashed over his worried face. Eluding the conductor's grasp, he darted toward her.

"Please, Missee, save Coya!" he pleaded pathetically. "Don't let them send me back to my cruel father!"

CHAPTER III

A Strange Visitor

The girls regarded the lad from India with troubled eyes. He was such an appealing character that they longed to help him, yet they wondered if they would be doing right to aid him in running away from the circus.

"Where do you wish to go, Coya?" Nancy inquired gently.

"Coya has no choice," the boy smiled. "Wherever new friends go—that might be a nice place."

"I live at River Heights. But if I should pay your fare there, then what would you do?"

"Coya work—cut grass, feed chickens, wash dishes. Oh, the hand of Coya is very willing. But I pray you, send me not to Rai, for he is cruel and his heart is black."

Nancy held brief consultation with Bess and George. The three were agreed that they did not want to send the boy back to a man who whipped him so mercilessly. Finally they paid his fare to River Heights, inviting him to sit with them at the front of the car. In truth they were a little worried, for they knew they

could not conscientiously abandon Coya when their destination should be reached.

"I'll take him home with me for a day or two," Nancy whispered. "Of course we'll have to communicate with the circus, but perhaps Father can arrange matters so that Coya will be happier than he has been."

Upon hearing the remark the Indian lad's face grew troubled, and the girls correctly guessed that he did not approve of their plan of notifying the circus in regard to his whereabouts. However, he offered no comment save to thank Nancy over and over for paying his fare. Whenever her eyes chanced to rest upon him he would smile worshipfully.

Coya's command of English was somewhat limited, the girls learned, and it was not easy to draw him into conversation. He seemed especially vague in answering their questions about his life in the United States. While his recollections of India were vivid, he could not recall when he had come to the United States or the age at which he had joined the circus. Rai had never talked to him of the past, nor had he permitted the lad to study English or talk with strangers. Although Coya did not say so, Nancy received the impression that Rai had been afraid the boy might learn too much concerning his former days.

Soon the River Heights water tower was sighted from the car window and the girls be-

gan to gather up their belongings. Coya, eager to show his appreciation for their aid, insisted upon carrying the heavy suitcases into the vestibule.

Nancy and her friends were the first passengers to alight when the train came to a standstill at the station. Scarcely had they stepped down to the platform when Nancy heard her name called.

Turning, she saw Ned Nickerson, a young man who attended Emerson University in a nearby city, coming swiftly toward her. He looked very handsome indeed in a well-pressed, gray suit of collegiate cut, and as always his eyes were for Nancy alone, although he greeted Bess and George perfunctorily.

"Why Ned!" Nancy exclaimed in delight. "I didn't expect to see you at the station!"

"Your father told me you were arriving today," Ned smiled warmly. "It's surely great to see you again, Nancy. You're looking like a million dollars!"

"I feel that way too, Ned. You don't appear to be run down yourself!"

"Oh, I manage to bear up," Ned grinned.

He stooped to grasp Nancy's suitcase, when for the first time he noticed Coya, who stood guard beside the luggage. The girls hastened to explain the Indian lad's presence.

"I don't know what Dad will think when he learns I'm bringing home this visitor," Nancy

confessed uneasily. "Is there room for all of us in your car, Ned?"

"We'll make room." Ned was amused at this latest escapade of Nancy, and he could readily imagine that Coya's unexpected arrival at the Drew residence might result in unforeseen complications, but he wisely refrained from expressing his thoughts.

Everyone squeezed into the automobile with Coya perched precariously atop the luggage. Ned stopped first at the Fayne residence and then at the Marvin house before taking Nancy home.

"Won't you come in?" she invited the young man as he assisted her to alight at her own doorstep. "I may need you to help explain matters to Hannah about Coya!"

"I'm afraid I can't stop this time, Nancy," he replied as he and the Indian lad carried her bags up the walk. "I promised Mother I'd do an errand for her. I'm late now."

Hannah Gruen, the housekeeper, had observed the automobile at the door. As Ned drove away she rushed joyfully out to greet Nancy.

"How glad I am to have you back home!" she exclaimed tremulously. "The house has seemed so quiet and empty——"

She broke off abruptly to stare at Coya. "Mercy upon us! Nancy, what does this mean?"

"Now don't get excited," the girl said soothingly. "Don't say another word until I've had a chance to explain."

"If this is another one of your jokes——"

"Coya is going to stay with us for a day or two. He ran away from the circus and when the conductor intended to put him off the train, I paid his fare."

As the lad went back to the car for more luggage, Hannah spoke her mind.

"Nancy Drew, you're talking in absolute riddles. But if you think I'll take a brown-skinned boy to raise, you have another think coming! There's enough work in this house without adding to it!"

"That's exactly the point," said Nancy, as the boy returned. "I thought Coya could help you. He could mow the lawn and take care of the garden."

"Coya scrub floors, too," added the boy with a winning smile, as he reached the porch. "Wash windows very clean."

"Humph! You don't look strong enough to do any real work," the housekeeper replied sternly, but her face softened. "I declare, you're nothing but skin and bones!"

"Coya has had a very hard life," Nancy said quickly.

"As far as I'm concerned, he may stay," Mrs. Gruen gave in, "but the matter isn't settled until your father agrees."

"I'll win Dad over," Nancy declared confidently.

While Coya was eating a substantial lunch in the kitchen, the girl told Mrs. Gruen in the living room everything she knew about the boy. As she had anticipated, the woman's sympathies were aroused.

"I do feel sorry for the poor little fellow," the housekeeper admitted, "but somehow I don't like the idea of taking him into the house. After all, you know very little about him, Nancy."

"We could give him the room over the garage. It's clean and nice. I'm sure it will be better than anything Coya had while he was in the circus."

"Have you thought what may happen when the boy's father learns we are keeping him here?"

"That's the one drawback, of course. Rai has an ugly temper and I'm afraid he may make trouble."

"You'll be accused of kidnaping, Nancy. Talk the matter over with your father when he comes home, but I rather think he'll decide that the boy must return to the circus right away."

Coya, realizing that his position in the household was far from assured, attempted to make himself as useful as possible. He immediately set about washing windows, polishing them until they gleamed like diamonds, and when he

had finished that task devoted himself to the garden.

"I never in my life saw such a good little worker," Mrs. Gruen admitted.

Nancy was unpacking her suitcase when it occurre. to her that she had not displayed her ivory charm to the housekeeper. She returned to the kitchen and began to relate the story connected with the carved elephant. Just then Coya chanced to come into the house for a drink of water. His alert eyes immediately fastened upon the trinket.

"Coya, do you believe that this charm has any of the powers Rai attributed to it?" Nancy asked curiously.

"Oh, yes, Missee! The ivory charm is wonderful—good luck will follow you. When Rai give it to you I tell myself it best I try to stay with new owner. That way good luck follow me too!"

"I hope you're right," Nancy laughed.

When Carson Drew came home that evening the girl gave him a detailed account of her meeting with Rai and was greatly relieved to find her father in sympathy with her desire to keep Coya.

"The boy is unusually alert and an excellent worker," he commented. "If you wish, I'll write his father and try to arrange matters so that we can employ Coya. It's obvious that Rai isn't a suitable person to look after him."

"Write the letter now," Nancy urged eagerly.

Mr. Drew obligingly complied with the request, but looked troubled when he was ready to address the envelope.

"The man must have another name besides 'Rai'," he said. "Mr. Rai doesn't look very well in print."

"I'll ask Coya," Nancy promised.

She returned a moment later with the Indian lad. When the matter was explained to him, he offered to address the envelope himself. Both Nancy and her father were surprised to note that he wrote a smooth, flowing hand.

"I will mail the letter, too," Coya added hopefully.

"Why, thank you," Nancy smiled. "The post box is at the corner."

Coya took the envelope and departed, but no sooner had he disappeared from view than he paused and withdrew the letter from his pocket. He stared at it a moment, then tore it into a dozen pieces, which he dropped into the gutter.

"This way I make certain Rai never find me," he reflected. "Now I stay always with my kind friends."

Unaware that the important missive had been destroyed, Nancy hopefully awaited an answer. With the elapse of several days she grew anxious. Coya seemed not to mind the

uncertainty of his future and appeared so care-free and happy that at times it occurred to her to wonder at his attitude.

When a week had slipped by and still no word was received from Rai, Mr. Drew attempted to trace the man. However, the Bengleton Circus had jumped from town to town, and for the time being could not be located.

One evening Nancy was sitting alone in the living room when the front doorbell rang. Hannah had left the house a few minutes earlier to visit a friend, so the girl arose to answer the summons.

Switching on the porch light, she opened the door. At first glance Nancy thought that the caller was a young woman. But a more careful survey convinced her that the stranger was at least fifty years of age, although she had skill-fully disguised the fact by the use of stylish clothing and the clever application of make-up.

"Is Mr. Drew at home?" the newcomer inquired.

"No, he is not in just now. But I expect him any moment. Won't you come in?"

"Yes, I believe I will wait. My name is Miss Allison—Anita Allison."

The woman followed Nancy into the living room, accepting a chair which was offered. She glanced quickly, almost nervously, about the room.

Nancy tried to place the visitor at ease but she could find no subject in which Miss Allison appeared interested. She was considerably startled when the caller asked abruptly:

"Do you believe in dreams?"

"Well, in a way yes, and in a way no," Nancy returned, purposely vague.

"I am dreadfully upset over one which I had a few nights ago. That's why I have come to consult your father."

"He isn't exactly a specialist on dreams."

"I want to talk to him about a legal matter— a property deal. You see, I inherited a large section of valuable land some time ago. Now a group of promoters wish to buy it for a golf course. They offered me an excellent price."

"Then I should think you would find their offer tempting."

"I do, but you see I had this dream. A strange man appeared to me and forbade me to go ahead with the deal. It upset me so that I decided to talk the matter over with Mr. Drew."

Nancy sternly restrained a smile. She knew that her father would be amused, if not annoyed, at such a silly attitude.

Before she could make any response to Miss Allison's remark, the woman uttered a choked little cry.

"What is that thing around your neck?" she demanded tensely.

Nancy's fingers went swiftly to her throat to touch the ivory elephant charm. She had forgotten that she was wearing it.

"Why, it is an Indian charm, Miss Allison," she explained, starting to remove the trinket from the velvet string. "Would you like to see it?"

"Would I like to see it?" the woman echoed, laughing hysterically. "You ask me——"

She arose from her chair, taking a step toward Nancy. Her thin hand reached out as if to snatch the trinket, then fell to her side again. The color drained from her face.

Before Nancy could move forward to assist her, Miss Allison sagged back into her chair in a faint.

CHAPTER IV

A Baffling Incident

Nancy moved swiftly toward the stricken woman, only to halt uncertainly as the front doorbell rang. She would have ignored it entirely had she not observed a man's face pressed close against the glass pane. She wondered if he had seen Miss Allison faint. At least he might offer aid.

Darting to the door, she flung it open. Without waiting for an invitation to enter, a tall, athletic looking man deliberately strode into the room.

"I am Steve Roach," he announced quickly. "Miss Allison's escort."

"You're just in time to help! Miss Allison has fainted."

The stranger moved swiftly to the chair where the woman lay in a crumpled heap, and to Nancy's amazement lifted her up in his arms.

"I'm very sorry this happened," he said apologetically. "Miss Allison is subject to fainting spells."

"I am afraid I may have said something to

29

excite her,'' Nancy returned anxiously. ''Will you please carry her up to a bedroom?''

''Oh, no, I'll take her to my car. She'll be all right in a minute or two.''

''But she's as white as a ghost. You shouldn't take her away in that condition.''

Miss Allison stirred slightly in the arms of her escort.

''You see, she's coming around now,'' the man said quickly. ''Please let me handle this in my own way. I understand Miss Allison's case far better than you do.''

Nancy realized that it would be useless to protest. She held the door open for Mr. Roach, and with troubled eyes watched him carry the limp figure to an automobile parked in front of the house. The man placed Miss Allison in the seat beside him and drove away.

As Nancy turned from the door, she noticed that the living room curtains had not been drawn. It occurred to her then that undoubtedly Steve Roach had been watching the house from his car and had observed Miss Allison's peculiar actions.

''I wonder if I should have permitted him to take her away?'' she thought uncomfortably. ''Everything happened so quickly I had no time to think.''

She felt convinced that the woman's fainting spell had been brought on by a glimpse of the carved ivory charm. Taking the trinket from

the velvet cord about her neck she studied it
intently. Surely it guarded some secret. Yet
about its mysterious nature she could not haz-
ard even a guess.

The brilliant beam of a headlight flashed
across the driveway at that moment and Nancy
ran to the window in time to see her father's
car enter the garage. She was relieved that he
had returned home and hastened outside to relate the strange events which had occurred during his absence.

"I never heard of anyone by the name of
Anita Allison," Mr. Drew said thoughtfully.
"And I'm certain there's no one in River
Heights called Steve Roach. Can you describe
him?"

Nancy furnished an accurate description of
the man but the lawyer shook his head. It did
not fit any of his acquaintances.

"I can't understand it at all," he declared.
"Evidently they're a strange pair, to say the
least. I'm just as glad Miss Allison didn't remain to consult me, for I take no stock in silly
dreams and I might have offended her by saying so."

"It was odd that she fainted when she saw
my ivory charm."

"You're certain that was what brought on
the spell?"

"I'm not really sure, of course. But I know
she became greatly excited when she saw my

carved elephant. I believe she had seen it before.''

''That seems almost impossible.''

''Yes, it does. It isn't reasonable that she could be acquainted with Rai.''

''Perhaps the charm isn't as unusual as you believe, Nancy. It may have been duplicated many times.''

''Possibly,'' Nancy agreed doubtfully, ''but even so the charm must have some strange significance. I feel certain there's a mystery connected with it.''

''It's beyond me,'' Mr. Drew smiled. ''However, it will be interesting to see if anything develops.''

''I have a feeling that something will,'' Nancy returned earnestly. ''If Miss Allison should come to your office tomorrow, don't forget to do a little detective work in regard to the charm.''

''I'll try,'' Mr. Drew promised.

The following afternoon Nancy was gathering a bouquet of flowers from the garden when Ned Nickerson's car shot into the Drew driveway.

''Hello, Nancy,'' he called gaily.

''Hello, Ned. I see you've been in a smash-up.'' She indicated the fender of the front wheel which had been crushed out of shape.

The young man alighted from the machine

as he replied gruffly to the girl's statement:

"I'm disgusted about it, too!"

"Then you shouldn't drive so fast."

"I wasn't traveling even twenty-five miles an hour when the accident occurred," Ned protested. "It happened last night. I had the right of way. A big car barged out of a side street and struck my fender. The crash would have been a lot worse, only I managed to swerve."

"It's a wonder you weren't injured."

"Yes, this driver was as reckless a fellow as I have ever encountered on the road."

"Why didn't you have him arrested?"

"I had no chance. He didn't even get out of the auto."

"You mean he didn't stop to learn if you were hurt?"

"He stopped for only an instant. I asked him what he meant by crashing Benton Boulevard and he cut me short by tossing a ten-dollar bill out the car window. 'That should be enough to keep you quiet,' he yelled at me. Then he drove on."

"You didn't take down his license number?"

"No, he was gone in a flash. But I'll recognize the fellow if I see him again. He was tall and dark—the athletic type."

"At what hour did the accident occur?" Nancy asked quickly.

"Around nine o'clock."

"Why, that was about the time Steve Roach left our house last night," Nancy said, half to herself. "And he was traveling toward Benton Boulevard."

"Who is Steve Roach?"

"A stranger who called at our house. Tell me, Ned, was the driver alone?"

"No, he had a lady with him. She was pale and sick looking. I thought she had been crying, too."

"Would you judge her to be of middle age?" Nancy questioned with growing excitement.

"Well, she looked fairly young to me. She was stylishly dressed."

"Anita Allison does appear young at first glance," Nancy said.

She quickly related her experience of the previous evening, and her description of the two visitors tallied perfectly with Ned's own observations.

"Perhaps the fellow was excited because of Miss Allison's illness," he remarked doubtfully. "Even so, that was no excuse for his acting the way he did."

"What sort of car was Roach driving?"

"I didn't notice the make. It was fairly new, painted green, and had tan wheels."

"Such a car should be pretty easy to spot again."

"I'll be on the watch for it at any rate," Ned replied grimly. "Then ten dollars will

just about pay for the fender, but I'll not feel
satisfied until I've given that fellow a piece
of my mind!''

''He's rude by nature, I think, Ned. At least
he acted rather high-handed at our place last
evening.''

''I guess the best thing I can do is to keep
the ten dollars and forget about it,'' Ned smiled.
''I really came over to ask you to go to the ball
game.''

''I didn't know there was to be one.''

''River Heights has a crack team. This
should be a good game. Want to go?''

''I'd love it.''

''We'll have to hurry. The game is called
for two-thirty sharp.''

Pausing only long enough to tell Hannah
where she was going, Nancy sprang into the
car and the couple drove rapidly toward the
ball park. Leaving the automobile not far from
the entrance gate, Nancy and Ned joined the
throng which was milling toward the ticket
window.

Suddenly the girl heard her name called. The
next moment George and Bess bore down upon
the pair. After chatting for a few minutes Ned
went to buy tickets for them all.

''It will be lots more fun sitting together,''
George declared enthusiastically. ''Everyone
says the game should be one of the best of the
season.''

Nancy did not reply, for her attention had been attracted to a large, green automobile which had just entered the grounds.

"I do believe that is Steve Roach's car!" she exclaimed.

Ned, returning with the tickets, arrived in time to hear the remark and catch a glimpse of the machine in question.

"I'm sure it was the same one that struck my car last night!" he cried.

Waiting for no further confirmation of her identification, Nancy darted through the crowd ahead of her companions. As the driver alighted from his car she saw that she had made no mistake. He was indeed Steve Roach!

Nancy spoke his name and added urgently, "Tell me about Miss Allison. Is she feeling better today?"

The man turned quickly, yet regarded Nancy with a cold, blank stare.

"My name is not Roach," he denied. "And Miss Allison? I am sorry, but you have made a mistake. I am acquainted with no one by that name."

CHAPTER V

The Door in the Rock

Steve Roach's denial of his identity did not mislead Nancy. She was firmly convinced that he was the same man who had called at her home the previous evening.

However, before she could press the matter, Ned and her chums came hurrying up. As Roach recognized the young man, an angry, embarrassed flush stained his face, and his attitude became defiant and surly.

"Well, what do *you* want?" he questioned sharply.

"I think you know," Ned returned coolly. "You owe me an explanation for your actions last night——"

"I owe you nothing, you young upstart! Didn't I pay you ten dollars just for a few scratches to your fender?"

"If you think it was only a few scratches come over and take a look at the car."

"I'll not be hounded over such a ridiculous matter," the man snapped. "And I have more important business just now than to stand here and waste time arguing with you. That's all

I have to say. But if you're wise you'll not annoy me again.''

Without giving the youth an opportunity to reply, Roach stepped back into his automobile. In his haste to drive away he barely avoided a group of women who were crossing the road. With frightened screams they leaped aside just in time to keep from being struck.

''That man must be half crazy!'' Ned cried furiously. ''I have a notion to follow and have him arrested!''

''You'll never catch him now,'' Nancy said. ''By the time you get your car he'll be a mile away.''

''And we'll miss the ball game,'' Bess added. ''It's time for it to start now.''

Ned allowed himself to be persuaded to give up the chase. The four friends entered the grandstand just as the River Heights team took the field and a few minutes later the umpire uttered his command:

''Play ball!''

The game was an exciting one with the two teams tied at 1—1 until the ninth inning. However, at times Nancy found her attention wandering. She kept thinking about Steve Roach, speculating upon why he had denied knowing Anita Allison.

In the ninth inning River Heights broke up the ball game by scoring three straight runs. Nancy, Bess, George and Ned cheered lustily

at the result for they were loyal to the town team.

As they were driving toward home a little later, George suggested that it might be fun to have a picnic the following afternoon.

"Why not?" Nancy agreed enthusiastically. "The weatherman promises that it will be another nice day."

"I'm afraid I'll not be able to go," Ned said regretfully. "I don't expect to be in town."

"I suppose we could make it a girl-only picnic," Nancy suggested. "But I think Coya might like to go. He's had no fun since he came to work for us."

"We could take him along anyway," Bess declared. "He would come in handy to lift the heavy hampers." Bess liked to eat.

"Three girls shouldn't need such heavy baskets of food," Ned teased. "Not if they mean to keep their girlish figures."

After some discussion the picnic definitely was scheduled for the following day. George brought up the question of where it should be held.

"Let Nancy name the place," Bess suggested. "She always knows of such unusual sites."

"I don't know any new place offhand," Nancy said, "but I'll try to think of one before tomorrow."

She really gave the matter no more consideration until later that evening when a chance

remark by her father at the dinner table re-
called the subject to mind.

"I have a bit of information which may interest you," Carson Drew commented. "It
concerns your new acquaintance—Anita Allison."

"She came to see you?"

"No, but a real estate dealer dropped into
my office today and from him I gleaned a little
information regarding the woman's property.
I learned its location. The land is considered
valuable."

"Where is it?"

"You remember the old Dawson farm east
of the city?"

"Yes."

"Well, Miss Allison's property adjoins it.
The land includes several acres of forest, a
river, beautiful rolling hills, a ravine, and very
nearly everything essential to a good golf
course."

"I believe I remember the place," Nancy
mused. "It would make an ideal spot for our
picnic tomorrow."

"I didn't know I was supposed to go on a
picnic tomorrow," Carson Drew smiled.

"You're not. This one is exclusively for
George, Bess and myself. And Coya, if you
are willing to spare him from his duties."

"By all means take him along," her father
urged. "The boy deserves an outing."

The next morning shortly after eleven o'clock, Bess and George, laden with thermos bottles and hampers, arrived at the Drew residence. Nancy and Coya were in the back yard loading the automobile with their own picnic equipment.

"We have enough food for an army," George laughed. "Ned was right when he warned us that we would lose our girlish figures."

Soon the little party was on its way. Nancy, drove directly east through the city.

"Where are you taking us?" Bess inquired with interest.

"To a new place," Nancy smiled mysteriously. "I think you'll like it."

The success of the outing seemed assured from the start, for little Coya fairly bubbled over with enthusiasm and his gaiety was imparted to the others. He loved the out-of-doors and amazed the girls with his stories of country life in his native land. He asked eager questions regarding the names of unfamiliar trees and birds. Nancy and her chums were slightly embarrassed when they could not always give an answer, and resolved to devote themselves to nature lore with new interest.

"I'm ashamed that I don't know the names of half the birds I see," Nancy confessed. "I intend to find a book at the library and study up about it."

Presently the car passed the Dawson farm. Following the directions given by her father,

Nancy turned into a narrow, winding side road which led between tall rows of elm trees and a tangled growth of shrubbery.

"I never dreamed there was such a place as this so near River Heights!" Bess gasped in awe. "Where *are* you taking us, Nancy?"

"To see Miss Allison's land. Don't you think it's an interesting picnic ground?"

"Ideal," Bess approved. "And this looks like a good place to stop, too."

She indicated a wide spot under a huge maple at the side of the road. Nancy parked the car and switched off the ignition.

"Coya will bring food," the boy announced with a broad smile. "Young ladies walk ahead and find place."

Nancy and her chums located a small opening in the fence and crawled through. They were delighted with the wild, natural scenery and stood for some minutes admiring the view from a cliff above the river. When Coya came with the first of the hampers, they selected a smooth knoll near by and spread out the luncheon cloth.

Soon the meal was ready, but as the girls prepared to sit down to partake of it Coya moved shyly away.

"He doesn't understand that we expect him to eat with us," Nancy commented in an undertone. "Coya!"

The boy's face lighted up as she beckoned

him to join the group. Nancy filled his plate with delicacies. Coya waited until everyone had been served before touching his food; then he watched Nancy's every movement, imitating exactly the way she handled her knife and fork.

"Coya learns American ways very rapidly," the girl thought. "His mind is so alert he really deserves a tutor. I must speak to Dad about it tonight. Perhaps he can arrange some studying."

After lunch the girls sat in the shade while Coya carried the empty hampers back to the car.

"It's nice having someone do all the work," Bess sighed blissfully. "If Coya lived at our house I'd be spoiled soon."

"We've grown very fond of him," Nancy answered. "If Rai should return to claim the boy now it would be disappointing." She abruptly arose and gazed thoughtfully across the river. "Can you imagine yourself standing here and driving a golf ball across the water?"

"I can't, because I don't play the game," George drawled. "My ball would go plop into the river."

"This place would have too many natural hazards to suit me," Bess added. "If I ever use this course I'd want half of the trees cut down."

"I imagine that old house would be torn down too and replaced by a handsome club building,"

Nancy commented, pointing to a large, apparently abandoned homestead, barely visible in the woods some distance away.

Bess and George both turned to stare.

"Why, I never noticed the place!" the latter exclaimed. "Do you suppose it belongs to the Allison property, Nancy?"

"It must. I'd love to explore it but of course we have no right. We're really trespassing as it is."

"At least it will do no harm to look at the outside of the building," Bess proposed. "Let's walk over."

"All right," Nancy agreed, looking toward the car. "I wonder what became of Coya?"

"Oh, he's around here somewhere," George answered carelessly.

The girls found a trail leading through the woods. Fortunately it took them directly to the abandoned homestead. Emerging into the tiny clearing, they were amazed to discover the missing Coya. He was standing on the front porch, apparently trying to raise one of the windows.

"Coya!" Nancy called sharply.

The boy wheeled. "Yes, Missee Nancy?"

"What are you doing?"

"No harm. Coya only look at old house."

"I fancied you were trying to get inside," Nancy smiled. "You have no right to do that, you know."

"Coya think nobody care," the boy replied evenly.

Nancy considered the subject closed and gave the lad no further thought, as she and her friends walked slowly about the house. The windows were all placed high above ground so that it was impossible to gain any impression of the interior.

"It's just an old, empty house, I guess," Bess said.

The girls returned to the front of the building. Coya had vanished.

"Now what became of him?" Nancy inquired with a trace of suspicion. "Do you suppose he dared to climb in that porch window?"

"Coya had a mischievous look in his eye when he said he thought no one would care if he investigated," Bess added.

"He's probably inside," Nancy acknowledged. "When he comes out I'll give him a severe lecture."

The girls sat down under a tree some distance away but minutes elapsed and Coya did not reappear. At length Nancy grew impatient.

"I'm going in there and drag him out! It's time we start for home."

She arose and sauntered over to the porch. Bess and George saw her raise the window and step through.

Five minutes elapsed; then ten.

"What can be keeping Nancy?" George asked in bewilderment. "I think it's time I go after her. Want to come along?"

"I'll wait here. Only if there's anything interesting inside, come back and tell me."

"I'll return in three minutes," George promised.

She, too, vanished through the window. No sooner had she gone than Bess began to regret that she had permitted George to go alone. After ten minutes had elapsed she became convinced that something was wrong.

Hurrying toward the house she called loudly:

"George! Nancy!"

Her cries went unanswered. A sudden fearful conviction came upon Bess that Coya and her friends were being held prisoners inside the old house. If she were to enter she, too, might be captured!

"I'll go for help!" the girl decided.

Almost overcome with fear and anxiety, Bess raced down the trail toward the parked automobile. Once she stumbled and fell headlong, tearing her stocking. She scrambled to her feet and ran on again.

Reaching the car, she was relieved to find that Nancy had left her keys in the ignition lock. Yet when Bess tried to start the motor she had no success. Twice it caught, only to die.

She was about to give up in despair, when

at last her efforts were rewarded. Recalling that she had noticed a farmhouse at the end of a nearby lane, she determined to go there for aid.

She stepped hard on the gas pedal and the car leaped ahead with a jerk which flung her against the wheel. The thoroughfare twisted and turned in bewildering fashion and seemed to lead into the wildest sort of country. To the right, a short distance from the road, a high cliff loomed up.

For an instant Bess's attention wandered to the unusual formation. Then she stiffened, uttering a sharp, terrified scream.

Her imagination had not tricked her into believing that a portion of the boulder had moved. A man-made door, hewn in the solid rock, was slowly being pushed outward!

CHAPTER VI

THE HOUSE OF MYSTERY

TERRIFIED by the weird sight, Bess lost control of the steering wheel. The automobile careened wildly in the road, then pitched heavily into a rain-gutted ditch.

The impact momentarily stunned the girl. Recovering quickly from the shock, she was relieved to discover that the car still stood on its four wheels, apparently in an undamaged condition.

From the door in the rock a boy emerged. He ran down the steep bank toward the girl.

"Coya!" Bess screamed, and then laughed in relief. "For an instant I thought you were a ghost!"

"Coya no ghost. Very much real."

"You nearly made me kill myself."

"Coya very sorry," the boy murmured contritely. "You not hurt?"

"No, I'm all right, thank goodness. But I wonder if I'll ever be able to get Nancy's car out of the ditch?"

"Coya push and it be all right, I think."

"First tell me if I'm dreaming," Bess com-

manded. "Did I actually see you come through
a door in that boulder?"

Coya nodded, politely waiting for another
question before revealing any vital information.

"But you were investigating the abandoned
house when last I saw you!" the girl cried in
bewilderment. "How did you get here? And
what became of Nancy and George?"

"Coya see no one in tunnel."

"You've been exploring a secret tunnel?"
Bess demanded eagerly. "Does it lead from
the abandoned house?"

Again the Indian lad nodded. His brown
eyes danced with excitement as he tried to explain.

"When Coya step through window in strange
house find house have no insides."

"No insides? What do you mean?"

Coya seemed unable to make himself understood. He groped for words.

"You mean the house had no floor—no furniture?" Bess suggested.

"Yes, no floor, no insides! Steps lead down
into blackness. Then Coya fall. Find himself
at bottom of stone stairs. Long tunnel lead
here. Door open and rock push away."

Bess was bewildered at the boy's story, but
she felt convinced that his adventure offered a
clue as to what had become of Nancy and
George. Either in descending the stone stair-

way they had met with a mishap similar to the one Coya had experienced, or else had remained in the tunnel to investigate its strange character. Knowing full well Nancy's weakness for mystery, Bess was inclined to favor the latter theory.

"George and Nancy must be somewhere either in the tunnel or in the house," Bess declared. "Come, Coya, show me how to enter through the rock."

Obediently the little lad from India led the way up the steep bank to the boulder. He threw his shoulder against it and pushed, but the stone did not move.

"Strange," he muttered. "Most strange. Rock move easily when I push from other side."

"Let me help, Coya."

Although they both pushed with all their strength, it was impossible to budge the boulder even an inch. The secret door remained firmly in place.

"It's no use," Bess said in disappointment, giving up her efforts and resting. "Probably it doesn't open from this side. We must return to the abandoned house."

Remembering painful bruises he had received in the long fall down the stone steps, Coya hesitated, apparently none too eager to do this.

"Nancy and George may be in serious trouble," Bess said urgently.

"Then Coya go with you," the boy promised

I kept walking and stumbling in the dark until I came to a queer door in a rock. It sounds impossible but it's the truth.''

"I know it is," Bess agreed, "for I saw Coya emerge from that same boulder. He's been telling me a strange tale about the house having no insides."

"And that's the truth, too," Nancy declared. "It's the most fantastic, weird place I ever saw. Only I didn't see much of it! It was too dark."

"George must be lost somewhere in the tunnel."

"I'm afraid of that, Bess. We'll have to go back there and search for her."

"No need," Coya interposed earnestly. "Wonderful ivory charm save her."

"I wish I could believe such good fortune," Nancy said. "Probably the wisest thing to do is to return to the boulder. George should emerge from there eventually."

Hastily returning to the exit of the tunnel, the three began their vigil. First, however, Nancy convinced herself that Bess and Coya were correct in saying that the mysterious door could not be opened from the outside.

Minutes elapsed and the lost girl did not appear. Bess and Nancy grew more worried, especially when they noticed that the sky was becoming overcast with black, rolling clouds.

"Bad storm coming," Coya predicted.

"And it will soon be upon us," Nancy agreed.

"I believe it's useless to wait here. Let's go back to the house and enter through the window."

Again the group retraced their steps down the road and along the forest trail, coming at last within view of the abandoned house. In the gathering darkness it looked even more sinister and awe-inspiring than before.

"I don't like the idea of going inside," Bess shivered.

"Neither do I," Nancy admitted truthfully, "but we must find George."

She moved boldly toward the front porch, with Bess and Coya following very reluctantly. Nancy paused to listen intently.

"It was only thunder," Bess said.

"No, I heard something——"

The sentence was never finished. From inside the house there came a terrific crash accompanied by the sound of glass splintering against a hard, metallic surface. Then silence.

CHAPTER VII

The Chamber of Horrors

"Don't go inside!" Bess pleaded frantically. "Please don't. Something dreadful will happen to you!"

Nancy paid no heed. Boldly she flung up the window and stepped through the opening to find herself on a narrow ledge. She was startled to hear a low moan directly below her.

"George!" she called. "Is that you?"

"It's all that's left of me," a faint voice groaned.

Trusting herself to the treacherous stone steps just below her, Nancy quickly descended. When her eyes became accustomed to the gloom, she found her chum lying in a crumpled heap at the bottom, surrounded by a circle of broken glass. Her arms had been cut in several places.

"What happened?" Nancy gasped, endeavoring to stop the bleeding with her handkerchief.

"Oh, I've had a horrible time!" George half sobbed. "I lost myself in a musty old passageway. When I couldn't get out, I tried to come back the way I entered. I reached the top of

the stairs and then I slipped. To save myself I clutched at something hanging on the wall. It wouldn't support my weight. Down I crashed with it on top of me.''

''Apparently you pulled loose a heavy mirror, George. It's a wonder you weren't killed.''

''I can vouch for the heavy part,'' George answered ruefully, rubbing her head. With Nancy's supporting arm about her she slowly arose. ''Did you ever see such a chamber of horrors?''

''I never did. Can you walk if I help you?''

''I think so.''

Cautiously groping their way, the girls climbed the steep stairway. George leaned heavily on her chum. Before they reached the entrance ledge, Bess thrust her head in through the open window.

''Nancy! George!'' she called fearfully.

''Here we are, directly below,'' Nancy shouted. ''Bring Coya and come in. George has been hurt.''

''I'm all right now,'' the Fayne girl insisted. ''Have a care,'' she added as Bess prepared to step through the window. ''The ledge is very narrow.''

Nervously her cousin entered the house, standing motionless on the tiny platform until Nancy could locate an electric switch. As the room was flooded with light an amazing sight met their gaze.

The house was indeed "without insides." The flooring had been torn away, and from the rafters of the ceiling there hung several swings and trapezes similar to those used in circus acts. Huge mirrors which reflected distorted images of the girls were suspended from the walls. A safety net, badly torn, stretched beneath the ropes and swings.

"What do you make of it, Nancy?" Bess inquired in awe.

"It looks to me as if this place has been fitted up by acrobats—perhaps by amateurs who are practicing to become professionals."

"And how do you explain the mirrors?" George asked.

"I can't, unless they're used to aid the acrobats in their practice."

The three girls for the moment had forgotten that Coya awaited them outside the building. Reassured by the flood of light from the windows, the boy now appeared at the entrance.

"Raining very hard outside," he announced irrelevantly.

"Then do come in," Nancy urged. "We'll all stay here until the storm lets up."

While Coya marveled at the strange sights, Bess and Nancy bound up George's cuts and rubbed her bruises to the best of their ability. They had no bandages available but ripped strips of cloth from the former's clean underskirt for the purpose.

"This isn't a very neat job," Nancy apologized. "Perhaps it will do until we can get home."

Left to his own devices, Coya began to test out the ropes and swings. Bess uttered a little cry of alarm as the boy came swinging through space, hanging by his knees from the bar of a trapeze.

"He'll be killed!" she exclaimed.

"Coya was reared in a circus," Nancy reminded her chum. However, she thought that the boy was entirely too venturesome and warned him to be careful.

"Remember, the safety net is broken," she cautioned. "And some of the ropes look very old and insecure."

"Coya be careful," he promised.

Outside the old house rain fell in torrents. The girls decided that it would be unwise to return to their car until the storm should abate.

"While we're waiting, I believe I'll do a little investigating," Nancy said.

"We may as well go along," George added. "I'm feeling quite all right now."

Leaving Coya to amuse himself on the trapeze, the girls descended the stairway and entered the secret tunnel.

"Why was it ever built, do you suppose?" Bess speculated.

"That's what I'd like to learn," Nancy answered. "I have a feeling that so far we've

not delved very deeply into the mystery of this place.''

At the entrance to the tunnel the girls discovered a tiny room which neither Nancy nor George had noticed upon their previous trip through the passageway. It was empty save for half a dozen steel lockers similar in type to those used in gymnasiums. They were heavily coated with dust and evidently had not been used for some time.

The locker room held slight interest for the girls. They soon moved on down the tunnel, coming presently to a turn-off. Nancy paused a moment to consider.

''I'm sure I must have taken the main branch before,'' she said. ''Let's explore the other one.''

The passage which she indicated was very narrow and so low that the girls were forced to stoop. Suddenly Bess halted, gripping Nancy's arm.

''What was that?''

''I heard nothing.''

''It sounded like a groan.''

''Nonsense!'' Nancy laughed. ''You must have imagined it, Bess. Not that I blame you. So much has happened that I easily could imagine it myself.''

Unwillingly Bess moved forward again, slightly in advance of her chums. She had taken less than a dozen steps when she stum-

bled over the inert figure of a man stretched across the floor of the tunnel.

"Water! Water!" he mumbled.

Poor Bess would have turned and fled but she could not do so, for Nancy and George, who were directly behind, blocked the path. They, too, were startled, yet both realized that the man had been injured and needed attention.

Nancy knelt down beside him, raising him to a sitting position. In the dim light she could distinguish only the faint outline of his face.

"Where are you hurt?" she asked gently.

"My head—I think it's broken. I was struck by a robber and dragged in here. But I'll get even! I'll fix him!"

Spent by the effort of speaking, the man dropped back against Nancy, a heavy weight in her arms. It was several minutes before she could rouse him again.

"Who are you?" she questioned. "Tell us your name and why you are in this house."

"I'm Jasper Batt. Old Batty some folks call me. I look after the property."

"You mean you're the watchman?"

"Yes, I've been here since Pete was fired."

"Can you describe the person who struck you?"

"No," the man muttered. "He sneaked up behind me. I have a good idea who it was, though."

"Tell me his name," Nancy urged.

"No," Jasper Batt muttered. "I'll get even with him myself. And I'll get back my papers, too!"

"Papers?" Nancy inquired alertly.

"Valuable documents entrusted to me by Rai."

"Rai!" the Drew girl exclaimed, believing that she had not heard correctly.

"I was to give the papers to Miss Allison when she came for them. If I don't get them back I'll lose my job."

"I'll help you recover them," Nancy said soothingly when she saw that the watchman was becoming excited. "Only you must tell me more about the documents."

"Nothing to tell," Batt murmured, shaking his head from side to side. "I'll get the papers myself! I'll get square with that crook!"

He struggled to his feet, only to fall back into Nancy's arms, exhausted by the effort to arise.

"Leave me alone," he muttered angrily. "Leave me alone. Go away before I lose my job."

"The poor old fellow is out of his mind," Bess whispered. "What shall we do?"

"We must go for help," Nancy decided. "We can't possibly carry him ourselves."

"Coya is strong," Bess said. "Let's call him."

The three girls hastened back to the main

tunnel and groped their way along until they reached the illuminated apparatus room where they had left Coya.

Hearing nothing, Nancy called the lad's name, but the only sound that came to her ears was the fluttering of a sparrow against a high window.

"Coya was here just a short time ago," she said, her brow wrinkling in a puzzled frown.

Then George gripped her chum's arm excitedly. She pointed to the overhead web of ropes used for the gymnastic routine of the aerialists. Entangled among them, like a fly in a spider's web, hung the limp body of the boy, Coya.

CHAPTER VIII

A Courageous Rescue

The girls were stunned momentarily by the shocking sight. They had no way of knowing how long Coya had been hanging unconscious from the ropes. His face was so ashen in hue that they feared he had strangled to death.

"We must go for help," Bess gasped, but even as she spoke she knew that it would take far too long.

Nancy's eye had been roving speculatively over the network of ropes. Several dangled from the rafters, one in close proximity to the entangled body of the little Indian boy.

If only she would be able to climb the adjoining rope she might be able to reach Coya and cut him loose! The plan of rescue was a daring one but she determined to try it.

"See if you can find a knife or any sharp instrument!" she commanded her chums tersely. "Look in the locker room; or perhaps Mr. Batt has a pocket knife!"

In vain the girls searched the locker room for a knife. They were about to give up in despair when Bess spied a rusty old saw which had been

left in a dark corner. Snatching it up, they ran back to the apparatus room.

During their absence Nancy had managed to climb the tricky ropes. Spent and gasping for breath, she was endeavoring to reach a cross beam directly opposite the rope from which Coya dangled. George and Bess watched nervously as the girl swung herself toward the structure. She secured a grip with her feet, pulling herself until she was able to transfer from the rope to the beam.

Without waiting to be told what to do, Bess and George tied the old saw to the end of the rope Nancy had abandoned, and the girl then pulled it up.

"Be careful, Nancy!" Bess warned fearfully. "If you lose your balance it means instant death. You're standing directly over the hole in the safety net."

Nancy did not need to be warned to use caution. She knew that one misstep would prove fatal. Yet if she were to reach Coya she must take daring chances.

Clinging to the rope for support and with her feet on the beam, Nancy leaned forward, reaching out until she was able to grasp Coya's jacket. She pulled the limp body toward her, lashing the boy fast to the cross beam. Next she grasped the rusty saw and severed the rope which had strangled him.

"Is he still alive?" George called anxiously.

The question momentarily distracted Nancy's attention. At the same instant a loud clap of thunder rumbled through the empty building, startling the girl so that she nearly lost her balance on the beam.

The fright left her weak and spent. She clung tightly to her meager support until she had recovered somewhat. Then she calmly went on with her work.

Using a rope which Bess and George swung up to her, Nancy tied it securely about Coya's body. Severing the fetters which held him to the beam, she slowly lowered the boy to the waiting arms of her chums.

When Coya, still unconscious, was safely at the basement level, Nancy quickly slid down one of the ropes to join her anxious chums.

"I'm sure he's dead," Bess whispered. "He's as white as a ghost."

Nancy knelt down, pressing her ear against the lad's chest. She could hear the faint beating of his heart.

"Coya is still alive, but he needs stimulants. If only we had some medicine!"

In their great anxiety for the life of the little boy, the girls had forgotten about Jasper Batt. They were startled now to see him emerge from the passageway, staggering as he walked toward them. His eyes held a wild, half-crazed expression which the girls did not notice.

"Ask Mr. Batt if he has any medicine on the

premises,'' Nancy urged her companions. She continued to work over Coya, encouraged by the fact that a tiny bit of color was returning to his face.

Bess and George accosted the old watchman, and after explaining what they wanted several times they succeeded in making him comprehend them. He led them to a medicine cabinet in a back room and allowed them to make their own selection.

After administering the stimulant, Nancy was encouraged to notice that Coya's heart-beat became stronger. Soon he stirred a trifle and his eyelids fluttered open. He murmured something in his native tongue; then, gradually becoming aware of the little group about him, he smiled at Nancy with recognition.

"You save me," he whispered weakly.

"Don't try to talk yet," Nancy told him. "Just lie still and rest."

Coya did not obey the order. His eyes fastened themselves upon the ivory charm which Nancy wore about her neck, and he said insistently:

"Coya's life saved because of marvelous elephant charm!"

"Don't try to talk," Nancy advised again.

For some minutes Coya remained quiet, gathering his strength. Then arousing, he indicated that he felt able to sit up.

The girls had paid slight heed to Jasper Batt,

knowing that he no longer needed their aid.
They actually had forgotten his presence until
he suddenly pushed forward roughly to face
Coya.

"Now I remember! It comes back to me!
He is the one who struck me!"

"Impossible!" George exclaimed impatiently.
"You don't know what you're saying, Mr.
Batt."

"Coya is a friend of ours," Bess added.

"Coya," the watchman repeated. Obviously
the name was unfamiliar to him. "No, he was
the one!" he insisted wildly. "He told the
other man to strike me."

"Only a moment ago you said that Coya
struck you," Nancy reminded him. "And at
first you declared that you did not see your attacker at all. You're hopelessly confused."

"This man was the one," the watchman mumbled.

"Why, he's not a man at all—only a boy of
twelve," Nancy cried. "Coya couldn't have
been your assailant."

"You are in league with him! You plotted
with him to steal my papers! Give them back
to me or I'll lose my job."

"The man is completely out of his mind,"
Bess murmured in an undertone. "Don't pay
any attention to him."

However, it was impossible to ignore Jasper
Batt, for he was in a quarrelsome mood, de-

termined to make trouble. No amount of argument or explanation could convince him that Nancy and her friends knew nothing of the mysterious papers which had been stolen from him.

"You're all my enemies," he accused belligerently. "If you didn't come to trick and cheat me, why are you here?"

"We came to this house for no dishonest purpose, I assure you," Nancy said soothingly. "We'll leave immediately."

"Oh, no you'll not!" the watchman shouted. "Not until you hand over my papers. Give them to me."

"I tell you I know nothing of your papers. Try to be reasonable, Mr. Batt."

"If you won't give them to me, I'll take them!"

The watchman seized Nancy roughly by the arm, endeavoring to thrust his hand into the pocket of her jacket. Bess and George, enraged, went to their chum's aid. The struggle lasted only for a brief time, as Jasper Batt had not fully recovered his strength. He fell back against the wall, gasping.

"As soon as he regains his breath he'll be after you again, Nancy," Bess said in despair. "What shall we do?"

"We must get away from here before he becomes violent."

Overhearing Nancy's remark, Jasper Batt

moved swiftly to the foot of the stone steps, believing that the girls intended to escape by means of an upper window.

"Oh, no you don't!" he sneered.

"We must slip out through the secret tunnel," Nancy whispered.

She aided Coya to his feet, and with George supporting him on the opposite side, the little party moved stealthily into the dark passageway.

CHAPTER IX

TALES OF INDIA

MIDWAY down the long tunnel, the girls paused to listen. They could hear no sound of footsteps from behind.

"I believe we gave batty Mr. Batt the slip this time," Nancy chuckled.

"Don't laugh until we're safely out of here," Bess shuddered. "What if the door in the rock won't open?"

This suggestion erased the smile from Nancy's face, and no further word was spoken by her until the passageway exit had been reached. She groped about in the dark until her hand touched the knob of the door. It opened readily, swinging slowly back on mighty iron hinges which had been drilled into the rock. When closed, the door fit so tightly that only a close inspection revealed its faint outline against the cliff.

"Strange the rock door opens from the inside only," Nancy remarked musingly as they all emerged. "Some time I intend to learn the explanation for it."

"I fear you'll come back here alone, then,"

Bess commented grimly. "I've seen all I care to of this house."

The storm had abated while the girls were inside the tunnel. Now, as they assisted Coya to the parked automobile, only a light rain was falling.

"How are you feeling?" Nancy asked the Indian lad as she helped him into the car.

"Much better, Missee. But Coya try no more tricks on ropes!"

"I should hope not! Only a miracle saved you from death. If we had found you even five minutes later——"

"No miracle," Coya insisted firmly. "Ivory charm save life."

"If I were you I shouldn't trust that piece of ivory too far," Nancy smiled. "As soon as we reach home you're going straight to bed, and have a doctor."

Coya offered no complaint, yet a slight grimace told the girls that the Indian lad took slight stock in the ability of medical men.

By the time Nancy and Coya reached home, the lad had made such a noticeable improvement that it seemed unnecessary to call in a physician. Hannah put the little boy to bed and he immediately fell into an untroubled sleep.

"I declare, Coya has wound himself around my heart," the housekeeper confided to Nancy. "I didn't realize how much he meant to me until this accident."

"We must begin to plan his future."

That night after dinner she brought up the subject of engaging a tutor for Coya, and as she had expected, Carson Drew instantly agreed that the suggestion was an excellent one.

"Select someone suitable and it will be perfectly satisfactory," he said. "I'll leave the matter entirely to you."

"It won't be easy to find the right sort of teacher."

"That's why I'm leaving it all to you," Mr. Drew reiterated.

"By the way, Dad," Nancy said after a moment, "did Miss Allison ever call at your office?"

"No, she never did."

"It seems odd that she didn't come back."

"She probably switched to another lawyer. Not that I care."

"I heard her name mentioned today in connection with Rai," Nancy told her father.

He glanced up with interest, and she launched into the strange tale which Jasper Batt had related regarding the stolen papers. Carson Drew already knew of his daughter's adventure at the abandoned home but in the housekeeper's presence Nancy had withheld a few vital details.

"You're certain you heard the names correctly?"

"Yes, I'm sure I did. I suppose Batt must

know Miss Allison well for probably she employs him to guard her property. But it's beyond my comprehension how Rai can be mixed up in it.''

''The man is supposed to be with a circus miles from here.''

''It's possible Jasper Batt was completely out of his head,'' Nancy admitted. ''He certainly talked and acted wild enough.''

''Even so, he must have heard Rai's name mentioned or he couldn't have repeated it.''

Nancy nodded. ''And another thing: When Batt first spoke of Miss Allison and his valuable papers he seemed fairly rational. It was later that he talked so strangely.''

''Perhaps the old watchman's mind will clear up and he can explain what he meant,'' the lawyer suggested.

''I thought I might run out tomorrow and talk with him again,'' Nancy admitted.

''If you do, be sure to take someone with you,'' her father cautioned. ''Batt may be harmless enough in his normal state but if he hasn't recovered from the blow on his head, he may give you some trouble.''

''I'll be careful, Dad.''

As it turned out, Nancy did not make the trip to the abandoned house the following day, for another matter occupied her attention. Later that evening Ned Nickerson dropped in for a few minutes at the Drew residence and after

hearing of Nancy's exciting adventure, learned also of her plan to provide Coya with a tutor.

"Why, I know just the teacher for you!" he exclaimed. "Professor Lowell Stackpole."

"It seems to me I've heard the name."

"Well, I should think so! He has taught for years at Emerson U and is known also as a traveler and connoisseur. He has made at least ten trips to India and collects all sorts of native artware. Professor Stackpole speaks several languages, too."

"Wouldn't he want more than I could afford to pay, Ned?"

"I couldn't say as to that. But I imagine if Coya interested him he'd not expect a very high fee. Would you like to have me talk with him?"

"Indeed I would, Ned."

"I'll see Mr. Stackpole tonight, and if the position appeals to him I can bring him around here to talk with you tomorrow afternoon. How will that be?"

"Fine," Nancy agreed, immediately abandoning her plans to visit Jasper Batt.

Early the next morning Ned telephoned to say that he had arranged an appointment with the noted professor.

"We'll come to the house at three o'clock," he promised. "Professor Stackpole wishes to talk with Coya before he decides about taking the position."

"But his fee——"

"Don't worry about that," Ned chuckled. "If Professor Stackpole takes a liking to Coya, I'm certain he'll arrange something which will be satisfactory."

Nancy was excited over the approaching interview and hastened to tell Coya of her plans for his future. The Indian lad expressed appreciation for her interest, promising that he would study faithfully.

"As long as you keep Ivory Charm I do whatever you wish," he smiled.

"And if I should lose the charm?"

"Then bad luck follow us both."

Nancy was not certain that she liked Coya's attitude; yet, while he was greatly influenced by the ivory trinket, she believed that he would try to please her even if she did not have it in her possession.

When Hannah Gruen looked over Coya's scanty wardrobe she decided that he had no clothes suitable for his meeting with Professor Stackpole. Accordingly, Carson Drew took the boy to a downtown store and bought him a completely new outfit. Immaculately scrubbed and brushed and garbed in the new suit, Coya amazed the family.

"Why, you look actually regal!" Nancy laughed. "I'm sure Professor Stackpole will be impressed now."

Promptly at the appointed hour, Ned and the instructor called at the Drew residence. Doc-

tor Stackpole was a kind-faced, white-haired gentleman of seventy years; yet he carried himself very well and his gait was that of a much younger man. His bright blue eyes glinted with interest as he shook Nancy's hand. She noticed that his gaze rested for a long moment on the ivory charm which she wore about her neck, but he did not speak of the trinket immediately.

At first the talk was general, pertaining for the most part to Professor Stackpole's adventures in India.

"It is the most fascinating country in the world," he told Nancy. "You would love the temples and the great bazaars where native wares are bartered."

"I wish I might go there some day," Nancy said wistfully.

"I fear you would find many customs and practices which would horrify you," Doctor Stackpole continued. "The caste system has led to many abuses. Then, too, in certain parts of the country the natives have no idea of sanitation. In the name of religion they bathe together in sacred pools, many of them suffering from loathsome diseases. This same water is used later for drinking purposes."

"I'm glad I live in the United States," Ned interposed.

"Some groups believe in reincarnation—that they are to be twice-born," went on Doctor Stackpole. "In some places children marry at

Stackpole nodded approvingly from time to time, and after the boy had been dismissed said warmly to Nancy:

"It will be a pleasure to instruct such a lad. He is unusually bright for his years, and I feel confident that he comes from a family of high caste. His English may be faulty but in his native tongue he speaks with poetic beauty."

While Hannah served tea and cakes Nancy timidly brought up the subject of payment for Professor Stackpole's services. The gentleman named a sum so low that she felt inclined to protest.

"I tutor only because I enjoy the work," the teacher explained. "If Coya had not interested me, I should have declined the task."

Before Doctor Stackpole left the house arrangements were made for Coya to begin his studies the following day. Nancy accompanied the Indian boy to the professor's office where he secured a list of the books which would be required.

"Coya, you must study hard," she told him earnestly. "Kind Professor Stackpole will not bother with you otherwise."

"Coya burn much midnight oil," the boy smiled.

"If you learn other things as quickly as you do slang, I'm sure the professor will be highly pleased," Nancy laughed.

In the days immediately following Coya de-

doubted the story at the time the charm was given to me.''

"Very likely the tale is true," Professor Stackpole declared. "At any rate, your charm is valuable and should be safe-guarded.''

"I'll certainly take good care of it," Nancy promised.

"If you will call at my office some time I'll be glad to furnish you with several books dealing with the subject of charms," Professor Stackpole offered. "The ancient ones are especially interesting. Some of them are said to have contained precious jewels; others held a poison to be used against enemies, and a very few, a unique life-giving balm.''

"How would one ever tell the difference in the fluid?" Nancy asked curiously.

"The poison was dark in color, the life-giving balm of light hue. But of course, such things are of the past. The modern charms have no hollow cavities.''

Nancy had been fascinated by Professor Stackpole's tales of India, but she did not forget the actual purpose of his visit. Coya was summoned to meet the distinguished gentleman. The boy's bearing was beyond reproach. Upon entering the room he raised his right hand to his forehead and bowed respectfully to the professor. Then, seating himself cross-legged upon a cushion, he conversed with the teacher in his own language as well as in English. Professor

"Then ivory charms are somewhat common," Nancy observed in disappointment.

"It depends entirely upon the workmanship. Some are very rare indeed. If I am not mistaken, that charm which you wear about your neck came from India."

"It was given to me," Nancy said eagerly. "I've been very curious regarding its history."

"May I look at it?"

"I'll appreciate your opinion, Doctor Stackpole."

Nancy removed it from her neck and gave it to him for his inspection. He gazed at it so long without speaking that she began to fear it was merely a cheap trinket, nothing more.

"This is an unusual charm," he said at last in a tone which was almost reverent. "I have never seen one of better workmanship or quality. The ivory is pure, and I should judge very old. The carving has been done by an expert. Miss Drew, you have a treasure in this piece and should treat it as such."

"I had no idea it was so valuable."

"Unfortunately, I am not an ivory expert," the teacher said with a slight frown, "yet it is obvious even to one of my slight experience that this charm at one time must have been the possession of a person of high caste—perhaps a great Rajah."

"Rai claimed that it formerly belonged to a ruler of a mystic Indian province. I rather

an early age. A girl unmarried at fourteen would be considered a disgrace to her family.''

''I suppose certain natives place great faith in charms and omens,'' Nancy commented.

''Indeed they do. You might say that many of them are very superstitious. They believe in all sorts of miracles and sacrifices. Some religious groups hold the cow to be sacred, others the white elephant. Many wear amulets and charms to ward off disease, preferring such protection to the services of a doctor.

''The compounding of love charms is a standing source of profit. And there are natives who claim to have ability in Black Magic. They make clay images of those whom they wish to injure, thrusting spikes into them to cause illness.''

''I'm particularly interested in the strange beliefs held in connection with elephants,'' Nancy interposed.

Again Professor Stackpole's eyes wandered to the charm worn about the girl's neck.

''Of course you know that the Indians divide elephants into castes as they do people,'' he explained. ''The cult of the white elephant practiced by the kings of Siam probably had its origin in India and was based on the Hindu worship of Airavat, the sacred elephant of India. Even today one finds many charms made in the form of the elephant. Some are carved from pure ivory.''

lighted everyone by devoting himself to his studies with great zeal. When he was not working about the garden, he would retire to his room over the garage, where he could often be heard reciting his lessons aloud.

One afternoon, as she entered the garage for a garden tool which had been left there, Nancy was amused to hear the boy's familiar chanting voice. Coya was reciting a history lesson.

Then gradually the tone of his voice changed, and in a dreamy, sing-song chant, the lad began a strange, senseless jargon, apparently envisioning himself as the ruler of a great province in India. Nancy looked troubled when she left the garage and mentioned the matter to Hannah.

"I do hope Coya doesn't start to day-dream," the housekeeper commented anxiously. "I am afraid the boy is a bit off in regard to his imaginary ancestors. When I'm here alone in the kitchen he often comes in and tells me the most outlandish tales about his parents—how important they were in India."

"Professor Stackpole believes that Coya comes from a fine family," Nancy said thoughtfully. "I doubt that Rai is of high caste. I wish we could locate the man and question him."

Since the Indian had vanished with the circus and had not chosen to communicate with Mr. Drew, the task of tracing him would prove difficult. Nancy decided not to ask her father's aid in the matter until after he had finished

with an important law case which was causing him considerable anxiety.

She reflected that it might be well in the meantime to visit the abandoned house again and question the old watchman regarding his knowledge of Miss Allison and the man Rai.

Recalling her promise not to go alone to the house, Nancy telephoned to Bess and George. She was pleased that they had recovered from their recent unpleasant experience and were willing to re-visit the scene of their fright.

Early in the afternoon the girls drove to the Allison property, parking as near the empty house as possible. They circled through the woods toward the building and emerged from among the trees. Nancy, who was in the lead, halted abruptly.

Directly in front of the house, engaged in earnest conversation, stood a man and a woman.

"It's Anita Allison," Nancy whispered. "But the man is a stranger. Who can he be?"

tense voice. "Now I remember. We were talking about a——"

"White ivory charm," Nancy finished eagerly.

She became aware that Miss Allison no longer was gazing at her. The misty brown eyes were fastened upon a faraway hillside, and a strange expression came over the woman's face. As if in a trance she began to murmur:

"The elephant—the sacred elephant. Yes, yes, we were speaking of it—Rai and I—the sacred elephant!"

From a handsome white beaded bag the woman removed a gold covered book. The girls could not take their eyes from it for they had never seen such a handsome looking volume. It was very small, and inlaid with semi-precious jewels.

They were further bewildered when Miss Allison began to read in a musical voice from the tiny book. The passages which she selected were elaborate, poetical translations from the ancient Sanskrit.

Bess plucked at Nancy's sleeve, whispering nervously.

"Let's get away from here. The poor woman must be out of her mind," she said.

"She has some sort of psychic obsession," George added in an undertone.

Nancy was equally disturbed by Miss Allison's queer actions, for she had never met a

person of her type before. However, the girl
had no intention of abandoning the scene. She
believed that by listening intently to the passages she might gain a valuable clue from them.

"Do read on," she urged Miss Allison as the
woman paused.

Bess and George were completely baffled and
a trifle annoyed by their chum's apparent ab-
sorption in the Sanskrit translations. They
could make nothing of the passages themselves,
and after trying to listen for a time they grew
bored.

"I think Nancy has gone into a trance, too,"
Bess whispered to George. "Let's go off by
ourselves until she recovers!"

They slipped quietly away. Neither Nancy
nor Miss Allison noticed their absence. The
reading continued. Nancy was not bored. She
listened absorbed, for the excerpts, which
seemed to have been taken from an ancient
Hindu legend, related the tale of an Indian
prince who had been spirited away from his
parents. With her usual ability to make shrewd
deductions, Nancy had gone directly to the heart
of the situation.

"This story Miss Allison is reading must
have something to do with the Ivory Charm,"
she reasoned swiftly. "And I believe it has
a connection with Rai and Coya."

Nancy had not forgotten Jasper Batt's hint
that Miss Allison and Rai were acquainted.

She considered it very possible that the woman might know of Coya's parentage.

Despite the claims of the circus man, Nancy had never believed that Coya was his son. It occurred to her now that the Indian lad might be a person of regal birth, who, through the machinations of Rai and Miss Allison, had been stolen from his own country as a royal babe so that another might rule in his stead.

At first thought the idea seemed fantastic, yet Coya's own imaginings tended to give substance to the theory. Moreover, Miss Allison in her mutterings spoke frequently of a little-known province of India. Nancy ventured to inquire the name of its ruler.

"Maharajah Iama Togara," Miss Allison murmured dreamily. "He will rule with far more wisdom than will the boy Coya. I have read it in the sands of time."

At this significant scrap of information Nancy turned to look at her chums. She was surprised to discover they had gone.

"Tell me, Miss Allison," she asked quickly, "is Coya of royal birth?"

Before the woman had an opportunity to reply there came an irritating interruption. Jasper Batt emerged from the house, walking directly toward the pair. Observing the man, Miss Allison seemed to recover from her trance-like state. She closed the gold-covered book and hastily replaced it in her purse.

"Is Coya of royal birth?" Nancy repeated her question hurriedly.

Miss Allison's eyes had lost their faraway expression. Now she regarded the girl with a cold, impersonal stare.

"I'm sure I don't know what you're talking about, Miss Drew."

By this time the watchman had approached close enough to recognize Nancy.

"Oh, it's you!" he exclaimed in a quarrelsome tone. "I suppose you've come to make trouble!"

CHAPTER XI

TRESPASSERS

UNAWARE of the reason for Nancy displaying such interest in the Sanskrit readings, George and Bess wandered some distance from the abandoned house.

"Suppose we take another look at that door in the rock," George proposed suddenly. "I imagine it might open from the outside if only we can discover the secret."

"Nancy may want to return home soon," Bess said doubtfully.

"Oh, she'll be listening to that woman for a long while yet. I never thought Nancy would take stock in such psychic nonsense."

The girls walked rapidly through the woods. Selecting a more direct route than the one which followed the road, they soon emerged at the high cliff. Even at close range the door in the rock was not visible but they knew its exact location and readily traced its indistinct outline.

"There doesn't seem to be a single thing to push or pull," George commented after running her hand over the entire door. "It just isn't supposed to open, I guess."

Scarcely had she spoken, when the two girls were startled to hear a slight clicking sound which seemed to come from within the rock.

"What did you do then, George?"

"Nothing. My hand wasn't even near the rock."

George and Bess fell back a step, staring in amazement. The door was slowly swinging outward. Before they could recover from their surprise, a tall, muscular man emerged from the opening. He stood framed against the dark interior of the tunnel, holding the door to prevent it from closing behind him.

"What are you doing here?" he asked gruffly.

"Why, nothing," George stammered.

"You must leave instantly."

As George and Bess turned to retrace their steps along the forest trail, the man commanded sharply:

"Not that way!"

Closing the door in the rock, he indicated that the girls were to follow him. He led them directly to the road.

"Follow this to the main highway," he instructed, scowling. "And never come here again without written permission from the owner."

Bess and George scurried down the road, at the first bend pausing to glance back. The man had not moved from his position. He was still watching them.

"Now how are we to find Nancy?" Bess asked when they were out of sight. "She'll be waiting at the house for us."

"If she doesn't return to the car we'll have to double back and take a chance of being caught."

"I'd not care to meet that horrid man a second time. George, doesn't it seem to you as if we've met him before?"

"Not to my knowledge. Still, his face was somewhat familiar. I was too nervous to look at him very closely."

"I'm certain I've seen him before, George. Oh, now I remember! It was that man we met at the ball park!"

"Steve Roach! You're right, Bess. He wore different clothes today, but I believe he's the same person."

"Nancy said he was a friend of Miss Allison, too," Bess continued. "Apparently, he has taken it upon himself to protect her property."

The girls had reached the parked automobile. They paused there and were debating their next action when a figure emerged from among the trees.

"Nancy!" Bess exclaimed in relief. "We were worrying about you."

"And I've been engaged in a similar pastime," Nancy smiled. "I had no idea what became of you."

Bess and George quickly explained where

they had gone and told of their unpleasant meeting with Steve Roach.

"That man won't keep me away from here if I choose to come again!" Nancy declared with a quick toss of her head. "I doubt that Miss Allison ever gave him the authority to order people away from the property."

"I wish you had been along with us," Bess said. "We were so startled that we scarcely defended ourselves at all."

"I'd like to talk with Mr. Roach."

"Perhaps he's still at the cliff," George suggested.

Nancy glanced at her wrist watch. "It's late now and we really should be getting back to River Heights."

"Did you manage to see Jasper Batt?" Bess inquired as they climbed into the car.

Nancy laughed ruefully.

"I certainly did! And in a most unexpected way!"

"Don't keep us in suspense," George said impatiently. "What happened?"

"While Miss Allison and I were talking Jasper Batt came out of the house and accosted me. He arrived at just the wrong moment for the woman was just on the verge of revealing some important information."

"Did the man accuse you again of stealing his papers?" Bess asked with a smile.

"Oh, yes, he made a scene. I don't know what

Miss Allison thought of it all. Anyway, I managed to quiet him after a time and then I came to search for you and George."

"What is this information Miss Allison was about to reveal?" Bess questioned as the car turned into the main highway.

"Oh, she wouldn't say another word after Mr. Batt appeared. It was provoking. I thought she was going to tell me something important about Coya's parentage."

In response to the questions of her chums, Nancy went on to state her theory regarding the manner whereby the Indian lad had been brought to the United States.

"It's an interesting idea," Bess commented. "Is that the most you can say for it?"

"W-e-l-l," Bess hesitated, unwilling to offend her chum, "the theory is so startling it's a little hard to accept. But the case does have some baffling angles to it."

"I'm only starting to work on it," Nancy announced with relish. "This is the most interesting mystery I have ever encountered."

"That's what you always say," George chuckled.

"Perhaps I do, but I believe you'll agree with me before we're through with this affair."

The car was speeding along an open country road. Nancy slowed down for a curve; then, to the surprise of her companions, she quickly put on the foot brake.

"Now what?" George demanded. "Don't tell me we have a flat tire."

Nancy smilingly shook her head. She indicated a large signboard in a field to the left of the road.

"See that poster, girls! A circus is coming to town."

"Not to River Heights," Bess said in disappointment as she turned to read the sign. "It's showing at Hanover the twentieth of this month."

"And that's only a day away," Nancy added. "But you miss the significant part."

"Oh!" Bess exclaimed. "It's the Bengleton Circus! That was the one Rai was with, wasn't it?"

Nancy nodded. "Girls, let's plan to attend," she urged eagerly. "I'm curious to learn if Rai is still in the troupe."

"I never turn down an invitation to a circus," George said cheerfully.

"I'd love to go," Bess added quickly. "Will you take Coya, Nancy?"

"I think not. His recollections of the circus are not very pleasant, and he seems to be afraid of encountering Rai again. I believe it would be wise not to mention the matter to him at all."

"Coya may see one of the posters," George suggested.

"I'll try to keep him close at home for the next few days."

After dropping Bess and George at a downtown department store, Nancy continued toward her own residence. She was in great haste to arrive, for this was one of the afternoons designated for Professor Stackpole to tutor Coya, and she wished to talk to the distinguished gentleman before he should leave the house.

As Nancy ran up the front steps, the man was politely bidding Mrs. Gruen good afternoon. The door behind him closed.

"Are lessons over so soon?" Nancy inquired with a smile.

"Yes, it did not take me long to hear them. Coya is a brilliant student."

"I'm delighted to learn that, Doctor Stackpole."

"The lad's mind never ceases to amaze me, Miss Drew. His knowledge of Indian history is astounding, and he seems to be well versed in the traditions of various royal families."

"I've often wondered if perhaps Coya doesn't come from such a family himself," Nancy interposed quickly.

She half expected that Professor Stackpole would laugh away the suggestion, but instead he regarded her soberly.

"That possibility has occurred to me, Miss Drew. Do you know anything of the lad's parentage?"

Nancy described her first meeting with Rai

and Coya, adding thereto a little of the evidence she had gleaned from Miss Allison. As she mentioned the Sanskrit readings and the name of Iama Togara, Professor Stackpole's interest increased.

"Iama Togara is a well-known ruler of a small but wealthy province of India," he explained. "As I recall, the man took the throne under rather peculiar circumstances, but the details have slipped my mind. If you wish I'll look up the data for you."

"I'd appreciate it, Doctor Stackpole," Nancy said gratefully.

The tutor bowed politely and took his leave. Before the man was out of sight, the front door opened and Coya emerged. Nancy glanced at him sharply, wondering if he had been listening to the conversation.

"What is it that you want?" she inquired as the boy regarded her with an intent gaze.

"Coya have sudden premonition!"

"Did you learn that big word in your English lesson today?" Nancy questioned, smiling.

Coya appeared not to hear her.

"I have strange premonition," he repeated impressively. "Strange vision. Coya see himself on way to India to rule as great Rajah! Great honor come to me through help of Nancy!"

"Whoever heard such nonsense?" a familiar

voice demanded from the doorway. "Forget your premonitions, Coya, and start polishing the family car! If you don't, I have a premonition you'll get no supper."

Hannah Gruen emerged from the house, broom in hand, and Coya, thinking that she intended to use it on him, hastily fled. The housekeeper chuckled as she began to sweep the front porch, yet her voice held a note of irritation as she said to Nancy:

"That boy is rather provoking at times. Imagining himself a king! The next thing we know, he'll think he's too good to work."

"He hasn't shown any disposition to shirk yet."

"Perhaps not, but I don't aim to let the germ take root."

After Mrs. Gruen had gone back into the house, Nancy idled about the garden until her father came home. Making certain that Coya was not within hearing distance, she told him about the Bengleton Circus showing at Hanover.

"If I can get away from the office, I'll run over with you," he promised.

"And perhaps you'd like to visit the abandoned Allison house?" Nancy inquired slyly. "It's on the way."

"All right," the lawyer agreed. "You've told me so many wild tales about the place that I admit I've grown curious."

Nancy was awake early the next morning. She helped Hannah prepare breakfast and then, while she was waiting for her father to come downstairs, she unfolded the newspaper. Casually her eye scanned the headlines. She uttered a startled exclamation which penetrated to the far corners of the house.

"Dad! Mrs. Gruen!" she called. "Just come and read this!"

CHAPTER XII

A Box of Treasure

"Dear me, what is it now?" Mrs. Gruen inquired, hurrying from the kitchen. "When you shriek like that, Nancy, you scare a body half out of his wits!"

"Just look at this paper," Nancy cried, thrusting it into the housekeeper's hand.

"It says something about two mail train robbers being captured. Is that what you mean?"

"No, no. You're looking at the wrong story. Here, the one about the fire."

By this time Carson Drew had come down the stairs.

"What's this about a fire?" he asked.

"Oh, Dad, the old house burned down last night!"

"There are a large number of old houses in the vicinity of River Heights," Mr. Drew smiled.

"I mean Miss Allison's place. You know, the house I've been telling you about all week."

"And good riddance in my opinion," Mrs. Gruen declared firmly, offering the newspaper

99

to the lawyer. "Now that the house has burned down maybe Nancy will forget about it. I declare, between her talk of solving another mystery and Coya's claim that he's a king, it's a wonder I don't lose my mind!"

"Speaking of fires, I think I smell something burning now," Mr. Drew said, sniffing the air.

"Oh, mercy! The bacon!" Mrs. Gruen turned and fled to the kitchen.

Carson Drew quickly scanned the newspaper account. According to the story, the blaze had started during the night and was of unknown origin. A passing motorist had called the River Heights fire department but before the engines could reach the scene the building had been destroyed.

"It's queer Jasper Batt didn't discover the fire in time to save the building," Nancy commented musingly. "Probably he wasn't even on the premises."

"From what you've told me of him, Nancy, he couldn't have been a very reliable watchman. Possibly the fire started from a match or cigarette which he dropped himself."

Nancy nodded soberly. "Or it may have been set deliberately by someone who wished to conceal forever the secrets of that house."

"I guess the place doesn't represent much of a loss to Miss Allison," the lawyer said. "It would soon need to be torn down, anyway."

"Oh, the house had no intrinsic value,"

if it occurred to her to wonder how Nancy chanced to be so well informed regarding the secrets of the tunnel, she refrained from saying so. Instead, she murmured impatiently:

"No, no, we cannot enter that way."

Fortunately the portion of the basement in which the stone stairway stood had not entirely burned and so was fairly clear of debris. In a short while Mr. Drew had dragged away the timbers blocking the passage.

"It isn't very safe to enter just yet," he cautioned Miss Allison. "One easily might be overcome by fumes or heat."

"The air in the tunnel will be cool and clear," she insisted. "I must save my treasures!"

"Then I'll go with you," the lawyer was compelled to offer. "But I feel that the undertaking may be a dangerous one. You girls remain here."

Bess and George looked relieved, for they had been eyeing the great smoking hole with misgivings. Nancy, on the other hand, could not bear to remain behind.

"You'll need me to help you," she said to her father.

"I'd prefer that you remain above, Nancy."

"It is no more dangerous for me than for you, Dad."

"Oh, well, come along," Mr. Drew said.

Leaving Bess and George behind, the three

swiftly descended into the tunnel. The fumes were even more unpleasant than they had anticipated. Both Miss Allison and Nancy were choking and coughing before they reached the cooler interior of the underground passage.

Miss Allison went directly to a secret branch-off. She groped her way along until she located a rectangular stone set high up in the wall. Her hand moved deftly over it to touch a hidden spring.

Nancy and her father heard a faint click. Then the woman tugged at the block and it slipped outward from its place in the wall. In the cavity were several small boxes.

"Your treasures seem to be safe where they are," Mr. Drew commented. "I doubt that anyone would ever suspect such a clever hiding place."

"I dare not leave the boxes here," Miss Allison declared. "They must be taken to a bank vault."

"Well, that may be the best thing to do," the lawyer admitted. "It shouldn't take us long to remove the boxes."

He lifted several of them to the floor of the passageway, noticing their weight. It occurred to him to wonder what might be the nature of the contents, but Miss Allison offered no information and he tactfully refrained from asking her.

Nancy bent down to pick up a small package, only to have Miss Allison say quickly:

"No, I'll take that one."

So the girl selected another box, her father lifted one of the heavy cartons, and with Miss Allison bringing up the rear, they started with their burdens down the tunnel.

Carson Drew, who was in the lead, suddenly halted. As yet Nancy and Miss Allison had heard no unusual sound. Suddenly a loud, rumbling noise thundered through the tunnel, and a few loose stones overhead came clattering down dangerously near their heads.

The lawyer pushed his daughter and Miss Allison back against the wall, saying sharply:

"Don't move!"

They huddled there for several minutes until the stones had ceased to fall. A thick cloud of dust filled the passageway.

"There's been a cave-in somewhere ahead," Mr. Drew said tensely. "Let's get out of here before we're buried alive."

"We can't leave my treasures behind!" Miss Allison cried in distress as she saw that Mr. Drew intended to abandon the boxes. "They represent a fortune!"

Considering the emergency, Nancy and her father thought that the woman was somewhat selfish to place her own interests above their lives, but knowing that it would take less time

to carry the boxes than to make Miss Allison understand the need for haste, they resumed their burdens and hurried down the tunnel.

They were able to go only a short distance. Rounding a slight turn in the passageway they were dismayed to find it blocked by a pile of dirt, rock and overhead beams which had given way during the cave-in.

"I was afraid of this!" Mr. Drew exclaimed. "We're trapped!"

"Oh, what shall we do? What shall we do?" Miss Allison wailed. "We'll never get out of here alive."

Sinking down on one of the boxes of treasure, she sobbed hysterically.

"The situation probably isn't as serious as it appears," Mr. Drew said with forced cheerfulness. "If we're unable to dig our way out, Bess and George may soon realize that something is wrong and send help."

"The cave-in doesn't extend very far!" Nancy cried. She had been pulling and tugging at one of the half-buried timbers. "We're near the main tunnel entrance and I think I can see a faint streak of light!"

"You're right, Nancy," Carson Drew agreed jubilantly. "We may get out of here by our own efforts yet!"

The two fell to work with a will, succeeding after some time of back-breaking labor in slightly enlarging the aperture. But beyond

that point they could not budge the heavy
beams.

"If I only had a few tools we'd soon be out
of here," the lawyer said in disappointment
as he sank down on the floor of the tunnel to
rest. "As it is, I fear we're trapped. We
must wait for a rescue."

Nancy measured the opening with her eye.
"I believe I could crawl through, Dad."

"You're not large, Nancy, but you're not
that small, either."

"If you'll help a little I think I can make it.
I'll try, anyway."

Before Mr. Drew could protest, Nancy thrust
her head and shoulders into the yawning hole.
Midway through she wedged fast. She
squirmed and twisted, unable to move either
forward or backward. Then by sheer strength
Mr. Drew pushed her through to the other side.

"Now I'll help you and Miss Allison," Nancy
called back.

Her father's muffled voice came to her from
the opposite side of the debris.

"We could never make it. Go for help."

Nancy ran to the main tunnel and was relieved to find it clear. She raced up the stone
stairs, accosting Bess and George who were idly
regarding the ruins.

"Come quickly and help!" Nancy pleaded,
"Miss Allison and my father are trapped in
the tunnel."

"Trapped?" Bess gasped.

"Yes, in the branch-off. There was a bad cave-in."

Thoroughly alarmed, Bess and George followed Nancy down into the tunnel. For half an hour they worked like beavers trying to dislodge rocks and timbers. Without tools, the work progressed at a slow pace.

"We're all nearly exhausted," Nancy admitted at last. "I must go for help."

She ran back to the entrance, there to encounter Ned Nickerson, who had driven out to the Allison property to view the burned building.

"I thought for a minute that you were a ghost arising from the wreckage!" the young man exclaimed.

"Oh, Ned, we need your help," Nancy cried. "Dad and Miss Allison have been trapped by a cave-in."

Upon learning of the disaster, Ned did not waste precious moments asking useless questions. Grimly he followed Nancy down into the tunnel and set to work. The girls could have embraced him from sheer joy when he presently heaved aside the huge beam which barred the opening.

Miss Allison, pale and shaken, was lifted through, then Carson Drew followed.

"We must take the boxes," the woman mur-

mured weakly. "I'll not stir from this passage without them!"

To quiet the woman, Ned climbed back into the hole, handing out the heavy cartons one by one to Carson Drew. The girls helped to carry them from the tunnel.

Unaware of the importance of the task, Ned handled the smaller boxes a trifle carelessly. In depositing the last container, he allowed it to drop heavily on the ground. The cover of the box split open, and the contents, a collection of semi-precious stones, flowed in a tiny river of sparkling color over the grass.

"Oh, my treasures from India!" Miss Allison shrieked in anguish. "Save them!"

"Gee! I'm sorry," Ned muttered. "Why didn't someone tell me I was carrying jewels?"

He turned apologetically toward the woman and was dismayed to see her sagging toward the ground in a faint.

CHAPTER XIII

Following Clues

NED caught Miss Allison as she fell, easing her gently to the ground. The woman's eyelids fluttered open as Nancy and her chums bent over to minister to her, but she did not appear to recognize them.

"The treasure!" she whispered. "My precious treasure!"

"It is safe. Don't worry about it now," Nancy said kindly.

"Ned and I will take the boxes to a bank vault for you if you wish," Mr. Drew added.

Miss Allison did not appear to comprehend. A dazed, far-away look came into her eyes and she muttered incoherently.

"What is the matter with her?" Bess whispered anxiously. "I never saw anyone act like this before."

"I think she's going into a trance," Nancy declared.

As minutes passed and Miss Allison made no effort to arouse herself from the state of semi-stupor, Carson Drew grew impatient. He was half inclined to believe that Miss Allison made

no effort to control her nerves and actually tried to create highly emotional scenes.

"Something must be done about the treasure," he observed to Ned. "I suggest that we take the boxes to a bank vault while Nancy and the girls remain here with Miss Allison. If the woman isn't better by the time we return we'll summon a doctor."

The strange lady paid scant heed as the jewels which had fallen out on the ground were gathered up and replaced in the broken box. Ned and Mr. Drew carried all of the crates and cartons to the lawyer's automobile, returning to ask Miss Allison the name of her bank. She did not appear to understand the question.

"Where shall we deposit the treasure?" Mr. Drew asked. "Have you any preference as to a bank?"

"Please don't trouble me now," Miss Allison murmured indifferently. "I am meditating."

Finally, after several attempts to discuss the matter, Ned and the lawyer gave it up in disgust. They decided to take the boxes to the River Heights National Bank, and accordingly drove away.

Left alone with Miss Allison, Nancy and her chums tried to arouse the woman from her state of stupor. She paid no attention to anything they did or said until Nancy, hopeful of gaining information, deliberately mentioned Coya's name. The word seemed to arouse a

strange train of mental pictures in the woman's mind, for she began to mutter again.

At first the girls could distinguish nothing, but as Nancy bent over the relaxed figure, she caught enough to comprehend that Miss Allison was speaking of reincarnation.

"Gracious!" George exclaimed. "That's a theory of life, isn't it?"

"It's something to the effect that after death you'll be reborn as another person or animal," Bess said with a shudder.

"I imagine I'll be a goat!" George chuckled. "Or an animal equally attractive!"

"Sh!" Nancy warned, for she did not wish to miss a word of what Miss Allison was saying.

The woman lapsed into another silence, seemingly disturbed by the interruptions.

"You were just speaking of reincarnation," Nancy prompted quietly.

Miss Allison made no immediate response. Her eyes had focused upon the elephant charm which hung from its velvet cord about Nancy's throat. With trembling fingers the woman reached out and touched it reverently.

"The Ivory Charm will bring you good luck," she murmured. "Both in this world and the next. After death you will be reborn—you will enter a higher sphere and enjoy a life more splendid. You, Nancy Drew, will be reborn as a beautiful princess of India!"

"Oh, Nancy, please don't ask her another question," Bess pleaded, shivering. "I've never heard such dreadful talk before in all my life. It isn't *normal*. It frightens me."

"Don't encourage the woman to say such strange things," George added in a pleading whisper. "Just allow her to remain quiet until your father returns."

Nancy's curiosity had been whetted by Miss Allison's startling prediction. She longed to question the woman further, but with both Bess and George opposed to such a policy, she obediently submitted to their will.

Miss Allison lapsed into a moody silence. Presently she fell into a natural sleep from which she awakened in a quarter of an hour.

"Dear me, have I been sleeping?" she inquired, looking about in bewilderment. "Where am I?"

"Don't you recall the cave-in?" Nancy questioned in amazement.

"Oh, yes, now that you speak of it, I do."

"Surely you must remember that we carried out several boxes of treasure," Nancy reminded her, "and that a small box of jewels was dropped on the ground."

Miss Allison's blank expression made it evident to the girls that the incident had left no impression upon her mind.

"You remember nothing of what you said to Nancy?" George inquired incredulously.

Before Miss Allison could answer, Ned Nickerson and Mr. Drew, who had returned from their hasty trip to River Heights, joined the group.

"You're looking much better than you were, Miss Allison," the lawyer said.

"I feel quite my usual self, thank you. If you'll excuse me, I believe I'll go to my car now."

"Just a minute, Miss Allison," Carson Drew interposed. "Don't you care to hear what disposition we made of your boxes?"

"Boxes?"

"Yes, the treasure which we took from the tunnel. Ned and I deposited everything in a vault at the River Heights National Bank. Here is a receipt and your credentials."

Almost stupidly the woman reached out to accept the papers.

"Thank you," she murmured. "Thank you for your trouble." Abruptly turning, she walked swiftly down the wooded trail toward her car, which had been parked along the road.

"Well, is that all the appreciation we get for lugging her heavy old boxes?" Ned demanded gruffly when the woman had disappeared. "She made enough fuss about the treasure before we carted it to the bank."

"I don't believe Miss Allison is entirely herself," Nancy said. "She's been talking very wildly."

"I doubt that she understood what I was telling her," Carson Drew added with a troubled frown. "At any rate, I hope she doesn't lose those papers."

"Perhaps we can catch her before she leaves and explain matters again," Nancy suggested.

They all hastened to the roadside but Miss Allison had driven away. Mr. Drew consulted his watch and remarked that it was not too late to attend the circus.

"You'll come with us, won't you, Ned?"

The youth glanced quickly at Nancy, and upon receiving her eager affirmative signal declared that he would be pleased to join the party.

Hanover was crowded with automobiles, and the streets in the vicinity of the fair grounds where the huge circus tents had been erected were jammed with people, all traveling in the same direction. Carson Drew and his young friends joined the gay throng. Soon they heard the first strains of carnival music and were accosted by ticket-sellers, popcorn men, and vendors of red balloons.

"This will be heaps of fun and well worth the trip even if we don't find Rai," Nancy declared, skipping gaily along between Ned and her father.

"Are you quite certain that Rai wasn't just an excuse for the outing?" the lawyer teased.

Nancy shook her head. "No, I'll be bitterly

disappointed if we don't find him. We will, don't you think?''

"Now how should I know, Nancy? I haven't Miss Allison's psychic powers. I hope as you do that we'll be able to talk with the man, but he may be traveling with another unit of the Bengleton Circus.''

"I never thought of that," Nancy acknowledged, looking troubled.

"As I regard it," Mr. Drew said boyishly, "the main objective of this trip is to have a good time. So let's have it! We'll worry about Rai later."

Opening his wallet, the lawyer stripped off several bills and thrust them into Nancy's hand. "Take in the side-shows and buy all the pink lemonade you can drink! Ned and I will meet you inside the big tent. You'll find us by the monkey cage."

"By it, did you say?" Nancy laughed. "Or in it?"

The girls linked arms and strolled from one booth to another, listening to the barkers extol the merits of the entertainment within. Now and then they ventured inside, but usually were sorry that they had used up so much precious time.

"The circus will soon be starting," Nancy presently warned, looking at her wrist watch.

Even then they could not hurry as they moved along the lanes of caged wild animals.

They paused to study an ugly snake which lay coiled in its box.

"It looks a little like your old friend—the one who gave you such a loving squeeze," Bess teased Nancy. "And he's eyeing you speculatively now."

"Then let's move on," Nancy shuddered. "I don't trust that fellow."

The three girls elbowed through the milling throng, clinging to one another to avoid being separated. As they approached the monkey cage the crowd became even denser, drawn by the comic antics of the animals. It seemed hopeless to find Mr. Drew and Ned in such a mob.

"Oh, I see them!" Nancy cried presently. "Over there on the opposite side of the cage."

Before the girls could reach the pair, the crowd grew wildly excited, pushing and shoving in an attempt to move away from the vicinity.

"What's wrong?" George asked, clinging tightly to her chums.

Then she saw that a careless guard had left the monkey cage door unbolted and now a dozen of the mischievous little animals were escaping. One athletic fellow perched himself atop the cage, two others clung to the outside wire network, while the rest began to terrify the crowd by leaping from one person to another.

Nancy and her chums were tempted to laugh, until they found themselves being pushed and trampled by frightened spectators whose only thought was to escape from the scene. The excitement subsided somewhat when a band of guards arrived and by persuasion and force finally caged the truants.

Ned and Mr. Drew joined the girls at the first opportunity.

"Dad, I'm surprised that you'd deliberately unlock a cage door!" Nancy laughed. "Were you trying to get in?"

"At least no one has tried to feed me peanuts," Mr. Drew rejoined.

The circus was just starting and the party hurried to locate their seats. As they passed near one of the main rings where the show was in progress, a painted clown sighted Ned, and to the hilarious laughter of the audience pretended to pull a squawking live chicken from beneath his coat. The youth flushed in deep embarrassment and was especially annoyed because Nancy and her chums joined in the merriment.

Bess's chuckles were of short duration, for a moment later, as she hastily mounted the board seats, her slipper caught fast and before she could save it, tumbled to the ground some distance below. Ned gallantly went after the shoe and helped her to slip it on again. Before the two reached their seats they both felt that

they had supplied the audience with far more entertainment than had the circus acts which were in progress.

"I'm so humiliated I could die," Bess breathed as she squeezed in between Nancy and George.

"Forget about it and enjoy the show," George said. "No one is looking at you now."

The equestrian acts were under way and the girls were intrigued by the skill displayed by one youthful rider. The aerialists provided many thrills; the animal acts were interesting, though not as exciting as some they had witnessed at other circuses. Nancy began to stir restlessly in her seat.

"I wish the elephant act would start!" she declared.

"Seemingly your wish is to be granted," Mr. Drew smiled. "Here it comes now."

Nancy leaned forward in her seat, her eyes alight with expectation. This was the important moment for which she had waited. She caught a fleeting glimpse of the elephant trainer as he entered the big tent in full regalia.

"Is it Rai?" she whispered tensely. "It looks like him from here!"

CHAPTER XIV

A Bitter Disappointment

THE three jumbo elephants, guided by their trainer, had entered the ring directly in front of the section where Nancy and her friends were seated. The man turned to bow low to the audience.

"Oh, it isn't Rai after all," Nancy murmured in disappointment. "I was deceived by his costume."

"I was afraid we might not find him here," Carson Drew commented.

For Nancy, the circus entertainment had lost its zest. She paid scant attention to the elephant act, and when it was over whispered to her father that while the others were watching the remainder of the show, she intended to seek information regarding Rai from the circus manager.

After making inquiry from a worker who was scrubbing out an animal cage, Nancy was directed to the official's tent. He was busy at his desk and looked slightly annoyed as she entered.

"Anything I can do for you?" he asked

briskly in a tone which implied, "Please be brief."

"I came to inquire if you have an elephant trainer in your employ by the name of Rai," Nancy answered.

The manager pushed aside the papers on his desk, regarding the girl with interest.

"We did have," he answered. "Rai left the circus about ten days ago to search for a young charge of his who mysteriously disappeared."

"A boy named Coya?"

"Yes. Have you any information concerning him?"

"I might have," Nancy returned evasively. "Tell me, was Coya the son of this man Rai?"

"I'm not certain. He called the boy his son, but I was under the impression that the two were not related. However, he was greatly upset when the lad disappeared and insisted upon leaving the circus to search for him."

"Then Rai never received my father's letter."

"He received no letter offering any information about the boy. I am sure of that."

"I should like to ask another question," Nancy said. "Did you ever hear Rai mention a woman by the name of Allison—Anita Allison?"

"The name sounds familiar. I have a vague feeling that in some way the two were connected. Rai always did a lot of wild talking.

He often spoke of a mysterious treasure and it seems to me Miss Allison's name was mentioned in one of these tales.''

"Did you ever hear Rai speak of an ivory charm?''

The circus manager laughed ruefully. "Yes, Rai was superstitious. He believed in all sorts of evil and good omens. In some way he lost an ivory elephant charm, and whenever anything went wrong on the lot he claimed that it was because the piece was gone.''

Nancy was upon the verge of revealing that the trinket had been given to her, but the admission was never made, for just then a man appeared in the doorway of the tent to speak with the manager.

"Rai is back again,'' he announced. "The fellow wants his old job and insists upon talking with you personally.''

"Rai!'' the manager exclaimed. "Well, if that isn't a coincidence! Send him in.''

A minute later the Indian elephant trainer entered the tent. He bowed ingratiatingly to the manager, but the oily smile faded from his face as he observed Nancy.

"We meet at last!'' he said. "I have searched the far·corners of the state for you, and for my dear son Coya who has been taken from me. Tell me, what have you done with the Ivory Charm?''

"I still have it,'' Nancy admitted.

"Good! Excellent! You must return it to me, for since I gave the charm away my luck has been most depressing. Because I lost the ivory elephant my son disappeared."

"Coya ran away because you abused him," Nancy corrected.

"You dare to tell Rai that his son was abused?" the Indian cried angrily. "A beating now and then is good for a boy!"

"I have my own opinion, but I'll not argue with you. If you'll stand aside I'll return to my friends."

Rai's anger melted away but he made no move to permit Nancy to pass. His manner became fawning.

"We have no quarrel," he purred. "I can see that you are a young lady of great kindness and sympathy. Because of that you will not wish Rai to come to misfortune. You will give me back my charm?"

"I'll return it to you upon one condition."

"And what is that?"

"You must tell me the truth about Coya's parentage."

Rai hesitated and looked disturbed. Then he smiled.

"Certainly. The condition is easily met. Coya's mother died twelve years ago in India at the time of his birth. I, Coya's father, brought him to this country."

"You are not telling the truth," Nancy ac-

cused. "Unless you do, I shall keep the charm."

"I know no other story," Rai protested.

"Then I cannot return your ivory trinket." Nancy turned as if to leave the tent.

"Do not go!" Rai cried desperately. "I would gladly tell you what you wish to know if I were able!"

"Then you admit that I haven't learned the truth?"

Rai shrugged. "The truth? What is it? Who can tell? Perhaps Anita Allison might know, but she is far away."

"What was that you said?" Nancy questioned alertly.

Rai had not intended the girl to hear his words. Certainly he had no suspicion that she was acquainted with Miss Allison.

"There is only one who might tell you more of Coya," he answered vaguely. "She is beyond our reach."

"In that event there is nothing more to say, Rai. I must go now."

"But my charm!" the man cried frantically. "You will give it to me?"

"When you have fulfilled the condition I mentioned."

"But that is impossible."

"Then it is likewise impossible for me to return the charm."

"Wait!" Rai commanded as Nancy once

more moved away. "I will try to find a way.
I must see you again. We will talk of Coya
then."

"I will meet you whenever you wish."

"Then one week from today."

"And the appointed place?"

"I will write you a message."

"Very well," Nancy smiled, "I'll wait until
I hear from you."

She felt confident that Rai would not fail to
communicate with her, for his eagerness to
recover the Ivory Charm was almost pathetic.

Nancy thanked the circus manager for his
interview, nodded briefly to Rai, and left the
tent. She had walked scarcely a dozen rods
when she was startled to hear a workman utter
a cry of alarm. He ran toward her, waving her
back.

"Look out! Look out!" he yelled warningly.
"The elephants are stampeding! Old Tom has
gone on the rampage again!"

CHAPTER XV

Kidnaped!

Nancy scarcely had time to spring back and out of the way when the big elephant came charging angrily toward the manager's tent, the excited trainers in close pursuit. Others in the herd were milling about the lot or tugging nervously at their stakes.

"Get that man Rai away!" the keeper shouted. "Old Tom knows he's here. He hates him like poison and will tear up the place to get at him!"

As if knowing that his enemy was inside the manager's tent, Old Tom plunged straight toward it. Rai, white with fright, appeared in the doorway, took one swift glance at the oncoming elephant, then turned and fled.

Trumpeting in rage, Old Tom pursued him, bearing directly toward a group of children who stood in the path. With screams of terror the boys and girls scattered, all save one, who appeared too frightened to move.

"Look out!" the keeper shouted, starting to run in that direction.

Nancy knew that he was too far away to

126

reach the child in time. With no thought for her own safety, she leaped forward and jerked the little girl aside. Nancy herself stumbled and fell headlong.

"Don't move!" the keeper yelled. "Don't move!"

Nancy obeyed, remaining perfectly quiet as the elephant dashed by only a few inches from where she lay. Old Tom was so intent upon reaching his hated enemy, Rai, that he did not even notice the girl.

The Hindu fled toward the main entrance gate to lose himself in the crowd. The huge animal became bewildered, and when the trainers dug their hooks into his flesh and hosed him with water, he submitted to their will. Not until the beast was securely chained down did Rai venture to return.

"That elephant is dangerous!" the manager of the circus said to the keeper. "We'll have to get rid of him."

"Old Tom is all right," the other maintained. "He's the best elephant in the herd. Just keep Rai away from the lot and I'll have no trouble with him."

The circus folk had gathered about Nancy to praise her warmly for her courage in rescuing the child. For Rai they had only unspoken contempt.

When the excitement had subsided Nancy hastened back to search for her friends. The

circus performance had ended for the afternoon and the crowd poured out of the big tent. Carson Drew and the other members of his party, puzzled by the girl's long absence, had remained in their seats.

"What kept you so long?" Mr. Drew asked as his daughter mounted the board seats to join the group. "We were beginning to fear you had been eaten by a tiger."

"I was nearly trampled to death by an elephant," Nancy smiled.

"Tell us something we'll believe!" Bess laughed.

"It's the truth. Didn't you hear the noise and shouting outside?"

George shook her head. "The show went on the same as always. We did hear an unusual sound, but the band began to play just then and drowned it out."

"Old Tom, the elephant, went on a rampage. He seemed to know that Rai was here on the lot, and wanted to avenge himself upon him for his past cruelty."

"Rai!" Mr. Drew exclaimed. "Then he's still with the circus?"

"He came back today and is trying to secure work again. I doubt if he will, though, for after the cowardly way in which he ran from the elephant today he'll not be popular with the circus people."

Nancy then gave a more detailed account of

the trouble which had developed with Old Tom, and told of her conversation with Rai. When she spoke of offering her ivory charm to the man in payment for information regarding Coya, Bess cried out in disappointment.

"Oh, Nancy, you surely didn't give away your lovely charm!"

"I didn't, because Rai refused to tell me the truth. However, I gleaned a hint that Anita Allison is the person who has the real key to Coya's mysterious parentage."

"Perhaps we can arrange to see the woman tomorrow," Mr. Drew suggested.

"We don't know where she is staying," Nancy reminded him.

"No, it was a stupid oversight upon my part not to ask for her address. But they may have it at the bank—if she ever goes there to claim her property."

After idling about the circus grounds for some time, Nancy and her friends returned to their car. It was late afternoon when they started for River Heights. The roads were still jammed with automobiles and the trip consumed far more time than it should have. Consulting his watch, Mr. Drew announced that it was dinner hour.

"I suggest that we stop at the next eating place and have a bite," he proposed. "This will be my party."

The young people eagerly assented, for in

spite of the large quantities of peanuts and popcorn which they had consumed, they were still hungry. A half mile farther on Nancy noticed a brilliantly lighted inn just off the road.

"It looks as presentable as the average place we're apt to find," Mr. Drew commented, turning in at the driveway. "We may as well try it."

Entering the main dining room which was only half filled with guests, the party found a table for five near the window. After making her selection from the menu Nancy glanced curiously at the other diners.

"Why, isn't that Anita Allison?"

The others turned to stare.

"It is!" George agreed. "And she's with Steve Roach."

"I believe I'll go and speak to her," Nancy said impulsively.

"If I were you I'd not break into the conversation just yet," Mr. Drew cautioned. "Miss Allison and her friend seem to be engaged in an argument of some sort."

The couple talked earnestly together, totally oblivious of the other diners in the room. Their voices rose higher and higher until Nancy and her friends caught enough to deduce that the pair were discussing the sale of Miss Allison's property.

"The argument seems to be nearly over

now," Nancy presently observed. "If you'll excuse me, I'll go and speak to them."

"You might ask Miss Allison for her address," Mr. Drew suggested.

"I had intended to do that, Dad."

Nancy approached the table at the opposite side of the room and spoke Miss Allison's name. The woman started, and as she recognized the girl she made a pretense of welcoming her. Steve Roach scowled openly as he arose and offered Nancy a chair.

"I must apologize for interrupting your conversation," Nancy said. "I shouldn't trouble you except that I have a rather important matter to discuss with you."

"Perhaps another time—" Miss Allison began.

"Oh, I didn't mean that I wish to talk with you here, but I am eager to secure your present address so that I can find you again."

Miss Allison and her companion exchanged swift glances which were not lost upon Nancy.

"I move about from place to place," the woman answered vaguely.

"But you surely have an address. There must be some way to communicate with you."

"Just write a letter in care of 'General Delivery.' Then I can be sure of getting it."

Nancy was annoyed. She felt that the woman did not wish to give accurate information regarding her whereabouts. However,

realizing that it would be useless to pursue the matter further, the girl politely withdrew to her own table. Simultaneously Miss Allison and Steve Roach left the place without finishing their dinner.

"I don't like Miss Allison's attitude," Nancy complained to her father. "The least she could do would be to show a little appreciation for the way you and Ned saved her old treasure."

It was late when Carson Drew and his daughter reached home. They noticed a light burning in the room over the garage, and could glimpse Coya bending over his books.

Everyone was proud that the Indian boy was making such splendid progress with his studies. Professor Stackpole frequently boasted of his young pupil's ability, and these remarks were not always confined to Nancy or Mr. Drew.

The day following the visit to the circus Nancy wrote a long letter to Miss Allison in which she asked many questions concerning Coya's parentage. She frowned as she addressed the envelope in care of "General Delivery."

"If Miss Allison doesn't wish to answer she'll claim she never received the letter," Nancy told herself. "In sending this I feel confident I'm wasting my time."

The message was dispatched and temporarily forgotten.

That evening, while attending a party given
at the home of Mrs. Dreyfuss Winterhouse, a
River Heights society matron, Nancy chanced
to overhear Professor Stackpole speak of Coya
to his hostess, praising the boy highly. With
the best of intentions Mrs. Winterhouse a few
days later repeated the entire conversation to
Miss Allison, who happened to belong to the
same Cultural Club.

The latter listened intently, asked a few
questions, and by putting two and two together
shrewdly guessed that Coya had been living at
the Drew home since his mysterious disappearance from the circus. She immediately
communicated with Rai, telling him what she
had learned.

"Trust everything to Rai," the man responded grimly. "Within twenty-four hours
Coya will be in our hands again!"

Unaware that the boy faced danger, Nancy
and her father spent the following evening at
a moving picture show. Hannah Gruen likewise was absent from the house for she had
been called to the home of a relative.

At ten o'clock, when Rai stealthily approached the Drew residence, he instantly
noted that the place was dark. A light glowed
in the room above the garage where Coya was
studying his lessons.

For some minutes the man stood by the
shrubbery watching the boy at his work. Then

quietly he stole up the stairway to the lad's room. From his pocket he removed a drug-soaked handkerchief.

A creaking floor-board warned Coya of danger. He turned and saw Rai creeping toward him. Before the boy could utter a cry, the man sprang upon him, forcing the handkerchief against his face.

Coya struggled briefly, then relaxed into a limp heap. Chuckling wickedly, Rai slung the lad over his shoulder, and carried him down the stairway to a waiting car.

CHAPTER XVI

INSIDE THE COFFEE POT

SHORTLY after eleven o'clock Nancy and her father returned home from the moving picture show. As they ran the car into the garage they noticed that all was quiet in the room above. No light burned.

"For once Coya went to bed early," the lawyer commented. "Mrs. Gruen must be asleep too, for her room is dark."

Both Nancy and her father were weary, and they soon retired, never dreaming that any harm had befallen Coya. The following morning after Mr. Drew had gone to his office, the housekeeper requested Nancy to go to the garage to find out why the boy had failed to come for his breakfast.

"Like as not he's still sleeping," Hannah said irritably. "He sits up half the night studying. It's no wonder he can't get up in time for breakfast."

"Coya is usually so prompt," Nancy answered. "I'm sure he retired at a reasonable hour last night,"

"Well, I wish you'd see what is keeping him.

If he isn't here in five minutes he'll eat a cold breakfast!''

Nancy mounted the stairway leading to the garage room and knocked on Coya's door. Receiving no response she knocked again, and then, after listening for a sound, opened the door a crack and peered inside.

''Why, Coya hasn't slept in his bed!'' she exclaimed aloud.

Quickly entering the room she looked about in amazement. The bed covers had not been disturbed, revealing that the lad had failed to spend the night in his room.

The nearby table was cluttered with text-books and papers, the latter stained with a great blotch of ink from an overturned bottle. A chair too had been upset. A handkerchief lay on the floor. Nancy picked it up and sniffed at it suspiciously.

''Drugs,'' she murmured.

Next the girl's attention was drawn to a footprint near the doorway. It had been made by a large, muddy shoe. Nancy knew that Coya did not wear such a big size.

''The boy has been kidnaped!'' she thought. ''While we were all away from the house last night someone came here, drugged him, and carried him off!''

Nancy raced madly back to the kitchen to tell Hannah what had occurred.

''Coya has been kidnaped!'' she cried.

Mrs. Gruen's mixing spoon clattered from her hand to the floor.

"Yes. Come and see for yourself! The signs of a struggle are unmistakable."

Hannah followed the girl to the garage room, and readily acknowledged that the evidence had been correctly interpreted.

"This is dreadful, Nancy! Who could have done such a thing?"

"I have a suspicion, but of course no evidence."

"We must call the police at once."

"This isn't a case for the police in my opinion. I'll tell Dad what has happened. He'll know what to do."

Taking the car, Nancy drove directly to her father's office. The secretary informed her that Mr. Drew would not be in until after luncheon.

"This is his regular day at the municipal court, you know."

"Oh, I had forgotten," Nancy returned in disappointment. "I'll drop in again this afternoon."

Slowly she walked back to the parked automobile, seriously considering her next move.

"Nancy!" a voice called. "What are you doing downtown so early in the morning?"

She turned about swiftly, and her face brightened as she recognized Bess and George. It was the latter who had spoken. The two

girls were heavily laden with packages, mute evidence that they had been shopping.

"You look as if you were having trouble, Nancy," Bess observed. "Anything wrong?"

"Just about everything. Coya has been kidnaped. I can't reach my father and I feel that something should be done immediately."

"Have you called in the police?" George asked.

"No, I'll do that only as a last resort. I've decided to drive out to the Allison property and see if I can find Jasper Batt. I have a feeling he may know something of the matter."

"May we go?" Bess questioned eagerly.

"I wish you would! Jump in and we'll be on our way."

After a swift ride through the country Nancy parked the car as near as possible to the ruins of the old house, and then the girls walked the remaining distance. They were relieved to see Jasper Batt busy with a rake cleaning up the debris, for they had feared that he might not be available.

"I scarcely know how to approach the man," Nancy whispered nervously. "He may decide that I am an enemy again and attack us with the rake."

"We'll be on our guard," George declared. "If he seems to be in an ugly mood we can always turn and run."

The girls quietly drew near.

"Good morning, Mr. Batt," Nancy said
pleasantly.

The man looked up and scowled. "Well,
what do you want?" he demanded impatiently.
"Can't you see I'm busy?"

"I'll take only a minute of your time, Mr.
Batt. I want to talk to you about a boy named
Coya."

"I never heard of him. Go away and let me
attend to my work."

"Very well, if that's the way you feel,"
Nancy said, pretending to humor him. She
turned as if to depart, then paused again. "By
the way, Mr. Batt, did you ever recover those
valuable papers you lost?"

"No, I didn't!" the watchman snapped.
"But I know what became of them all right!"

"I suppose you lost them accidentally,"
Nancy said innocently.

"Lost them! I should say I didn't. They
were stolen by that no-good relative of mine.
He did it to get even with me because Miss
Allison gave me his job of taking care of the
place. Before I came here Pete was the watchman."

"Pete?" Nancy inquired.

"Peter Putnam," the man replied irritably.

"Let me see, he lives near here, doesn't he?"
Nancy probed.

"Too near to suit me. His place is about
twenty miles beyond Doverville. You won't

find Pete living in a regular house, though—not
that fellow. He's too stingy to build himself
a decent place. He lives in an old barn that
was standing on the property when he bought
it."

Nancy asked several additional questions,
but Batt became suspicious that he was being
pumped for information and lost all willing-
ness to talk. The girls returned to the parked
car without gleaning any new facts.

"I'd like to drive on to Peter Putnam's
place," Nancy suggested. "That is, unless you
girls are in a hurry to get home."

"Mother won't expect us for some time,"
Bess answered. "I'm in favor of pushing on
to see his queer house."

Half an hour's drive brought the girls within
the general vicinity of the Putnam farm, and
upon inquiry they were told to follow a winding, rutty lane which would lead them to their
destination. The property was located nearly
a mile from the main highway and consisted of
a few acres of cleared land completely surrounded by dense forest.

"This must be the place," Nancy commented,
halting the car near a strange structure which
resembled neither a house nor a barn.

The queer, tumble-down building originally
had been painted a brick red, but now appeared
to be a washed-out pink. A porch had been
erected at the front and large windows were

cut into the walls at uneven angles. An old silo, long since useless, adjoined the east side of the structure, while the west side supported a massive stone chimney.

"Did you ever see such a crazy looking house in all your life?" Bess giggled. "I wish I had a picture of it."

As the girls alighted from the car, a stout, short man in black corduroy trousers, sleeveless leather jacket, and a misshapen, dirty felt hat emerged from the building. Removing a brier pipe from the corner of his mouth he demanded gruffly:

"Well, what can I do for you? I warn you before you say a word that I'll not buy anything."

"We have nothing to sell," Nancy smiled. But she added shrewdly, "We might be willing to make a purchase."

"Eggs, or a chicken?"

Nancy shook her head. "I should like to discuss a business matter with you. May I come in?"

"All right," Peter Putnam consented gruffly, "but the place ain't fixed up much."

"We'll wait outside," Bess said hastily, speaking for herself and George.

Nancy followed the farmer into the house and tried not to stare as she noticed its dirty condition. The huge rooms were nearly barren of furniture. A cook stove, a kitchen table, and

a sagging cot comprised the main pieces. Peter Putnam drew up a box, offering it to Nancy in lieu of a chair.

"What is it you're willing to buy?" he asked eagerly.

"Perhaps I shouldn't have expressed it in just those words," Nancy countered. "I am searching for some papers which disappeared from an old house owned by Anita Allison. I am willing to pay well to recover the documents."

Putnam eyed the girl cunningly but he replied evasively:

"Now what should I know about any such papers? Pete Putnam tends to his own business."

"You were the former watchman at the Allison property. I thought you might be able to help me. As I said before, I am willing to pay well to recover the documents."

"Like as not that old rogue Jasper Batt stole 'em!"

"I think not."

"How much are you willing to pay for the papers?" Putnam asked cannily. "Mind I'm not saying I could get 'em back for you."

"I might pay twenty-five dollars," Nancy offered.

As she had anticipated, the sum sounded large to the miserly farmer. His face twisted into a grimace as he tried to decide whether

or not to acknowledge that the papers were in his possession.

"Well, if I learn anything about the documents I'll let you know," he said after a long pause.

Nancy had no intention of giving up so easily, but before she could think of a suitable response the two were startled to hear the angry barking of a dog in the yard. At the same instant Bess and George uttered a terrified scream.

Nancy rushed to the window. An ugly white and brown hound had cornered the girls near the house and with menacing snarls threatened to attack them.

"Call off your dog!" Nancy cried to Putnam. "Quickly! Before he bites Bess and George."

Seizing a whip from a hook on the wall, the farmer ran out the door. Nancy attempted to follow, but in her haste tipped over an old coffee pot which stood on a sagging shelf near the window. It clattered to the floor and the lid fell back to reveal a white object hidden inside.

Bending down, Nancy picked up the coffee pot. She removed a thin sheath of folded paper.

"What's this?" she thought, scarcely daring to hope that she had made an important discovery.

With trembling fingers she opened one of the papers and glanced at it. The document bore a fantastic gold seal.

"These must be the missing Allison papers!" she told herself. "What luck!"

It required but an instant to make sure. Then she thrust the precious documents into an inner jacket pocket. She replaced the coffee pot on its shelf, substituting an old letter at hand for the important papers which she had taken. Hastily she left the house.

In the meantime Putnam had driven away the hound, permitting George and Bess to escape to the automobile. Nancy joined them there, sliding quickly into the driver's seat.

"We must get away from here at once, girls! If Putnam discovers I've taken the papers he'll try to stop us!"

"The papers stolen from Jasper Batt?" Bess questioned eagerly.

Nancy nodded, triumphantly tapping her jacket pocket.

"I have the documents here. Let's hurry to a secluded spot where we can learn what they reveal."

CHAPTER XVII

A Vital Document

Several miles farther down the road Nancy drew up beneath the shade of an ancient oak, preparing to examine the papers which had been found in Peter Putnam's coffee pot.

"Isn't it a shame we didn't bring along a lunch?" she commented regretfully. "This is an ideal spot for a picnic and I'm as hungry as a Polar bear!"

"Would you be satisfied if I should offer you a peanut butter sandwich and a slice of chocolate layer cake?" Bess asked, smiling.

"Would I be satisfied? What a question! But you can't conjure up anything like that."

"Oh, can't I?" Bess laughed, reaching into the back seat of the car and lifting out a filled paper sack. "Here's a loaf of sliced bread, a jar of peanut butter, and a huge cake fresh from the bakery. I was taking the things home when George and I met you in front of your father's office."

"What will your mother say if we eat up the family provisions?" Nancy laughed.

"Oh, Mother gets hungry herself some-

times," giggled Bess. "We'll replace the items before we return home."

In high spirits the girls spread a blanket under a nearby tree and prepared for a feast, such as it was.

"We have no knife!" Bess exclaimed in dismay. "I never thought of that. How can we spread the sandwiches?"

"We'll use a nice clean stick," Nancy chuckled. "That willow tree should supply one."

"We can break the cake into big hunks," George added. "This will be fun. We'll use our fingers for everything."

While her chums labored over the sandwiches, Nancy opened the sheaf of documents, studying them eagerly.

"Don't keep them a secret!" Bess protested. "Did you get the right papers?"

"I'm sure I did. Some of these appear to be written in an Indian language, but others are in English."

"Is Coya's name mentioned?" George asked, peering over Nancy's shoulder.

"I haven't seen it yet. Yes, here it is! Oh, oh, it's just as I suspected all along!"

Nancy sprang to her feet, and to the amazement of her chums executed a little dance.

"Tell us what it's all about," Bess pleaded impatiently. "It's not fair to keep us in suspense. Either hand over that paper or reveal what it contains."

Nancy instantly grew sober, and sinking down on the grass she spread out the English document so that her chums could read it over her shoulder.

"I can't make a thing of it," George complained. "The writing is too cramped."

"It says here that Coya is the direct heir of a former ruler of an Indian province called—oh, dear, I can't even start to pronounce the place!"

"Don't try," Bess said. "Just give us the important details."

"As a babe, Coya was spirited away from his native land. Oh, I suspected it from the very first!"

"Why was he taken away, and by whom?" George questioned, trying to read the paper for herself.

Nancy studied the writing for several minutes.

"Girls, this is a shock! Coya was deprived of his throne through the work of Anita Allison!"

"Miss Allison!" George exclaimed incredulously. "But these papers belonged to her! Why did she not destroy such incriminating evidence?"

"I think I can answer that," Nancy said thoughtfully. "Rai gave these papers to Jasper Batt, who was to deliver them to Miss Allison. Before he was able to do so they were

stolen by Peter Putnam. Naturally, if Miss Allison had received the documents it's very likely she would have destroyed them immediately.''

"But how did the woman become involved in such a disgraceful affair?" Bess mused.

"One guess is as good as another," Nancy said. "But I'd judge it was through her interest in mysticism. At any rate, whatever her original motive may have been, she plotted to raise Iama Togara to the throne in place of Coya. This paper reveals that Miss Allison, working with Rai, kidnaped Coya. In return for making Togara a rajah, they received as their reward a priceless royal treasure. The natives were led to believe that the infant Coya had been devoured by a tiger; hence, they were willing to accept the new ruler.''

"It sounds fantastic," Bess declared.

"Rai couldn't have received very much of the treasure," George commented. "At least he appeared poor when we found him.''

"I imagine that Miss Allison kept the bulk of the loot for herself," Nancy said. "And just think! We helped her remove it from the secret tunnel.''

"Rai must be a stupid fellow to accept such an arrangement," Bess remarked. "One would think he would be inclined to protest.''

"He is no match for Miss Allison, that's certain," Nancy agreed. "I suspect the woman

kept him satisfied by giving him the Ivory Charm.''

"But why is the trinket so highly prized?"

"This document explains that the charm originally belonged to Coya's parents. It was one of the most cherished pieces in the family treasure and was believed to bring luck and health to the wearer.''

"Rai set great store by the charm,'' Bess nodded. "But he made a sad mistake when he gave it to you, Nancy.''

"Yes, Rai is sorry already that he parted with it. Unless I'm mistaken, Miss Allison will regret that she ever heard of that lucky piece before we're through with the case!''

"It may turn out to be her unlucky piece,'' Bess chuckled.

"There's one thing that worries me,'' Nancy said thoughtfully. "I believe that Coya has been kidnaped by Rai.''

"Surely the man can be traced,'' George replied. "He has probably gone back to the circus.''

"Harm may come to Coya before we can reach him. I feel certain that the boy will never remain voluntarily with Rai.''

"No,'' Bess agreed, "he will try to return to you, for he was happy living at your home.''

"Rai and Miss Allison are both afraid that Coya will learn of his true parentage,'' Nancy said slowly. "If they suspect that these papers

have fallen into my hands, the boy's life may
no longer be safe."

"You think they would be so heartless as
to put Coya to death!" Bess exclaimed in horror.

"I believe they might find a convenient
means of ridding themselves of him. We must
make every effort to find the boy before it is
too late."

The girls had been so intent upon their discussion that they had failed to note the approach of a small herd of cows pastured in
the field. A low, angry snort gave them their
first warning.

Startled by the unexpected noise, the girls
scrambled to their feet. Hurriedly they gathered up the blanket and picnic things. As the
unfriendly leader of the herd moved swiftly
toward them, Nancy and her chums rolled
under the wire fence which marked the bound-
ary line of the field.

"Just in time!" Bess exclaimed. "That
big red one meant to run after us."

Nancy abruptly paused and shook the blanket.

"My papers!" she cried. "Did either of
you pick them up?"

"Why, no," George answered. "Didn't
you?"

"I was so startled I don't remember. I
thought I did."

The girls hastily retraced their steps to the fence. Just beyond, lying in plain sight, were the documents.

"Nancy, you can't get them now!" George cried in alarm, comprehending her chum's intention. "You'll be injured!"

"I'm not going to lose those papers," Nancy replied grimly.

Jerking away from George's restraining hand, she rolled under the fence and moved swiftly toward the herd.

CHAPTER XVIII

DISCOURAGING DAYS

SNATCHING up the precious documents from the ground, Nancy raced back to the fence. George and Bess aided her to crawl through the wires.

"I guess those cows weren't as vicious as they looked," Nancy laughed shakily, as she carefully placed the papers in her jacket pocket. "Anyway, I had a bad fright about the documents, and it served me right for being so careless."

The girls were soon on their way back to River Heights. In approaching the Allison property Bess drew attention to an oncoming auto which had turned into the side road leading to the burned house.

"Few persons ever travel that way," Nancy said thoughtfully. "Do you suppose Miss Allison was in the car?"

"I couldn't tell so far away," Bess returned.

"Now that I know she is involved in the plot against Coya I must do everything in my power to locate her," Nancy continued. "Miss Allison ignored my letter and is making every effort to avoid me."

"It will only take a minute to stop and see who this person is," George suggested.

Nancy turned into the side road and soon drew up beside a sedan which had been parked near the burned house. The girls walked rapidly along the well-worn path until they came to the familiar clearing. There two men could be seen talking with Jasper Batt.

"I've never seen either of them before," Nancy commented. "I wonder why they are here?"

With one accord the chums moved forward until they could catch snatches of the conversation. It developed that the strange men were agents of the Reliance Insurance Company, sent by the local office to investigate the cause of the recent fire.

"Miss Allison is eager to have the claim settled as soon as possible," the girls heard Jasper Batt say urgently.

"I can well understand that," one of the agents replied dryly. "Unfortunately for Miss Allison the claim will not be settled, and she may consider herself fortunate if she avoids prosecution."

"What do you mean by that?" Batt demanded gruffly. "What has she done?"

"Our investigation discloses that this house did not catch fire accidentally. It was deliberately burned."

"You can't prove it!"

"Yes, Mr. Batt, our evidence will stand up in any court."

"You can't show that Miss Allison or anyone connected with her set fire to the house. It was probably done by a prowler."

"We are not through with the case," the insurance man replied grimly. "By the way, Mr. Batt, we have come here today to ask you a few questions. Where were you at the time the fire started?"

"Look here!" the watchman cried furiously. "You can't hang this thing on me. I don't know anything about it. I told you my idea of the fire—the house was burned by a prowler."

Chancing at that moment to glance up, Jasper Batt observed Nancy and her friends. His ruddy face became kindled with the light of an evil inspiration.

"Question those girls if you want to know who started the fire!" he exclaimed. "They are always snooping about this place. I suspect that they were the ones who struck me over the head and stole my papers!"

At mention of the word papers Nancy glanced uneasily at her companions. How well she knew that should the lost documents be found upon her person after such an accusation, explanations would not be easy to make! However, she walked boldly forward to speak with the insurance agents.

"Mr. Batt is not telling the truth," she said coolly. "My chums and I have no knowledge of how the fire started. The day before the house was destroyed we found Mr. Batt in an unconscious condition inside the building. He told us then that he had been struck over the head by an assailant who took his papers."

"That's the truth," Bess added earnestly. "Later, Mr. Batt began to accuse everyone of stealing the documents."

"Incidentally, he mentioned an old enemy," Nancy supplied adroitly, "a former watchman at this house named Peter Putnam. The two, I am told, were bitter rivals, and there was some bad feeling between them because Putnam was discharged by Miss Allison."

"It's a trumped up story!" Batt cried furiously.

The two insurance men had been impressed by Nancy's straightforward manner. They had dealt with persons of Jasper Batt's type before, and did not place great stock in the man's tale.

"What is your name, Miss?" one of the agents inquired.

"Nancy Drew. You may have heard of my father—Carson Drew."

"We certainly have! If you're his daughter there's no need for explanations."

"Then we are free to return home?" Nancy smiled.

"Certainly. We may need you later to offer evidence in the case, but in that event we'll call at your home."

"Thank you," Nancy said.

"You certainly walked out of that trouble adroitly," George praised, when the girls were on their way to River Heights. "I was afraid it might be discovered that you had the missing papers in your possession!"

"Jasper Batt was too stupid to think of such a possibility," Nancy chuckled.

After taking George and Bess to their homes she halted at her father's office to report to Mr. Drew the adventures of the day. He was deeply impressed with the documents which she spread before him and suggested that she show them to Professor Stackpole.

"That's an excellent idea," Nancy agreed. "I'll telephone now for an appointment."

After a brief wait she was connected with his residence, only to be informed that the man had left the city for a week-end visit.

"How disappointing!" Nancy commented as she carefully placed the documents in her father's safe. "Now I must wait until he returns."

"In the meantime we'll make every effort to locate Coya," Mr. Drew said. "Unless we find him again your papers will not be of much value."

Both Nancy and her father were confident

that it would not prove difficult to trace Coya. Their first act was to communicate with the Bengleton Circus. They were disappointed to learn that Rai had not returned to his old position.

Thinking that possibly the man had sought work with another traveling troupe, they made a complete canvass of the state. No one had heard of Rai.

"The search will prove more difficult than I anticipated," Mr. Drew admitted. "Obviously, Rai suspects that we may try to trace him and is hiding deliberately."

When Professor Stackpole returned from his trip Nancy lost no time in calling at his home. After relating the details of Coya's disappearance, she placed the important documents in the tutor's hands. He pored over them for nearly an hour.

"This is indeed amazing," he declared. "Amazing! Yet I cannot say that I am greatly surprised. From the first Coya impressed me as a lad of high caste and unusual ability."

"Then you believe the documents to be genuine?" Nancy inquired eagerly.

"Yes, I do not question them. In securing these papers, Miss Drew, you have accomplished a remarkable bit of detective work."

"I feel confident that Miss Allison is the person responsible for placing Iama Togara on the throne," she said. "These papers

practically prove it.   However, I should like to obtain an admission from Miss Allison's own lips.''

''But will that be possible?''

''I have a plan, Doctor Stackpole.   Will you help me?''

''I'll do anything in my power, Miss Drew. I am very fond of Coya, you know.''

''Then this is my scheme.   By some ruse invite Miss Allison here to your home.   You might pretend to consult her about Indian mysticism.   She will feel flattered at the invitation and accept it, I am sure.''

''And if she does accept?''

''Try to gain an admission from her that she helped to place Togara on the throne.''

''I fear I haven't your ability as a detective.''

''In this respect you will succeed where I would be certain to fail.   Miss Allison would never talk frankly with me.   She will be flattered by your interest.''

The scholarly man nodded thoughtfully. ''The plan might be worth trying,'' he said.

''With your permission I will hide near by and listen to the conversation,'' Nancy continued.   ''If Miss Allison refuses to talk, then I'll step out and confront her with the documents.''

''I shall attempt to make the appointment immediately,'' the professor promised.

Two days elapsed, and when Nancy received

no word from the tutor she began to fear that
he had failed. Then one evening he telephoned
her at her home.

"At last I have been successful in contacting
Miss Allison," he reported. "I made the appointment through my friend, Mrs. Winterhouse. Miss Allison has agreed to call at my
home on Tuesday of next week at three
o'clock."

"Excellent!" Nancy approved. "I will arrive ahead of her."

Impatiently she counted the many days which
would have to elapse before the scheduled
interview, and could not help but fret at the
delay. During them she devoted all of her
thoughts and energy to Coya's cause, or so it
seemed to Ned Nickerson.

"You need a little relaxation," he insisted.
"Why not attend the Omega Chi Epsilon house
party and dance at Emerson this week-end?"

"I don't feel a bit like dancing, Ned. Thank
you for the invitation, though."

"A day or so of fun would do you good,
Nancy."

"I'm not in the mood for it. I keep worrying about Coya. Why not invite another girl?"

"You know I'd never do that," Ned answered reproachfully. "You're the only girl
I want to take."

"There's one place you may take me,"
Nancy suggested.

"Where?"

"To the circus at Royalton. I saw it adver-tised yesterday."

Ned groaned. "We've attended every circus now within ten counties. I'm just about fed up with animals."

"So am I," Nancy admitted, "but I keep hoping that sometime I'll find Rai."

"I'll take you," Ned promised reluctantly, "but I'm sure it will be another wasted trip."

The prediction was a true one, for Rai was not located at Royalton or at any of the other circus towns which the couple visited. Oc-casionally, when Ned rebelled, George and Bess would accompany Nancy upon her searching tours. One afternoon as the three girls were returning after a discouraging day spent in a city some distance from River Heights, a large cross-country bus sped past them.

"Look! Look!" Bess cried, pointing toward a window of the vehicle. "Coya and Rai are in there! I caught a glimpse of them!"

Nancy did not question the identification. She quickly turned the car in the narrow road, but the bus had disappeared in a cloud of dust.

"You'll never catch it!" Bess exclaimed anxiously.

"Yes, I will," Nancy said grimly, pressing her foot firmly on the gasoline pedal. "I must!"

CHAPTER XIX

The Missing Elephant

Soon the bus was overtaken, but Nancy was compelled to follow it until it made its regular stop at the next town. As a few passengers alighted the girls eagerly scanned the faces of those still inside.

"I don't see anyone who resembles Rai," Nancy said in disappointment.

"He was sitting in a rear seat with a boy," Bess declared. "I'll step aboard the bus and see if they have changed seats."

She was back again in a moment, looking decidedly crestfallen.

"I don't understand how I made such a silly mistake. It's not Rai at all. Can you ever forgive me, Nancy, for starting you on such a wild chase?"

"Of course, Bess. It wasn't your fault."

"I'm awfully sorry. I was so certain that the man was Rai."

"Don't give the matter another thought," Nancy laughed. "This isn't the first disappointment I've had. But I mean to find Rai and Coya yet."

Later that evening Ned called at the Drew residence to learn the outcome of the trip. Nancy admitted that it had been a failure.

"I'm beginning to grow discouraged," she confessed.

"You need a little cheering, Nancy," he said coaxingly. "Why not come to the university week-end dance at Emerson? It will be a real party. The fellows are abandoning the Omega fraternity house and turning it over to the girls until the night of the dance. Mrs. Howard is to act as chaperon."

"I haven't any new party clothes to wear," Nancy said as she quickly thought of her wardrobe.

"Just pack any old thing. No one will notice," remarked Ned, man-fashion.

"Much you know of fraternity week-ends!" Nancy retorted. "All the girls will come dressed in their best. They'll have a gown for every occasion."

"They'll not hold a candle to you, no matter what you wear."

"You're very flattering," Nancy laughed. "I suppose I could go——"

"Then it's settled," Ned interrupted before she had an opportunity to voice another objection. "I'll write Mrs. Howard and tell her to expect you Friday evening."

Nancy did not regret accepting the invitation. By Friday her enthusiasm had mounted

to a high pitch, and as she motored with Ned
toward Emerson University she asked many
eager questions regarding the planned festivi-
ties.

"There will be enough to keep you interested," Ned promised. "Teas, and tennis,
a swimming party, and then the big dance."

Arriving at the fraternity house Nancy found
twenty girls already comfortably established.
After meeting Mrs. Howard, a pleasant,
motherly woman, she was introduced to her
roommate, a shy, timid girl who confessed that
she never before had attended such an affair.

"You'll love it," Nancy assured her.

The following day the girls were rushed from
one activity to another. Without making the
slightest effort, Nancy became popular with
everyone. She met so many new students that
she could not remember the names of half of
them. However, Ned's fraternity brothers re-
membered her, and that evening at the formal
party held in the chapter house they annoyed
the young man exceedingly by constantly
cutting in upon his dances.

"I think you've danced with everyone
here except Basha," Ned complained good-
naturedly to Nancy. "That's the punishment
a fellow gets for bringing a good looking girl!"

"Who is Basha?" Nancy inquired, paying
no heed to the compliment.

With a nod of his head Ned indicated an

Indian student, a handsome youth in evening dress who was standing at the opposite side of the room.

"I'll bring him over if you'd like to meet him."

"It might prove interesting," Nancy said.

Ned soon regretted that he had ever made such a suggestion, for after Basha had been presented he proceeded to monopolize Nancy's attention. He captured her interest by immediately mentioning the ivory charm which she wore.

"It is a remarkable keepsake," he declared. "I have seen none to compare with it—even in the collections of the mighty rajahs of my country."

The conversation continued at a furious pace, and poor Ned tried in vain to draw Nancy's attention to himself. She listened with an absorbing interest as Basha told of strange customs in India. The Hindu student in turn thought Nancy the most beautiful girl he had ever seen. It became increasingly clear to Ned that Basha was suffering from a severe attack of love at first sight.

At length the young man could endure it no longer. "Nancy and I have this dance," he told the Hindu. "It's time for you to scram!"

"Scram?"

"That's an English slang word meaning go —leave—depart. Unless you do, I'll be

tempted to challenge you to a duel at sunrise!''

''Very sorry,'' Basha apologized, smiling.
He bowed to Nancy and moved away.

Ned was not the only person present who
had noticed the Indian student's infatuation.
Some of the girls had overheard a part of
Basha's conversation, and teasingly inquired
if her ivory charm was responsible for such
popularity. Soon Nancy found herself dubbed
''The Girl with the Ivory Charm.'' She was
not certain that she enjoyed the notoriety, for
many persons asked to inspect the lucky piece.

She was tired when a waltz announced the
end of the dance. She went to her room,
tumbled into bed, and did not awaken until
the morning sunlight streamed in at the window.

Her roommate was already abroad, and
Nancy hastened to dress. Suddenly she became
aware that the ivory charm was no longer about
her neck. She tried to recall whether or not
she had removed it the previous evening before
retiring, but could not remember doing so.

She searched the dresser, the bed clothing,
her suitcase, and finally in desperation communicated her loss to the other girls. Everyone joined in the hunt, but the charm could not
be found anywhere in the house.

''Do you suppose that foreign student,
Basha, could have stolen it?'' a girl suggested.

''Oh, no!'' Nancy exclaimed instantly.

"But he was deeply interested in the charm. Everyone noticed it. And you said yourself that he spoke of its value."

Mrs. Howard, the chaperon, did not feel so confident that Basha was innocent. Unbeknown to Nancy, she telephoned the Hindu student, and after asking several rather pointed questions in regard to his knowledge of the charm, requested him to call at the chapter house as soon as possible.

A little after nine o'clock, Ned drove up hurriedly to the door and asked for Nancy. "I've just heard about you losing your charm," he said quickly. "But I'm sure Basha had nothing to do with the theft. The poor fellow is almost beside himself with worry. He thinks he is to be arrested. He's packing up his belongings now to leave the campus."

"I didn't accuse Basha," Nancy said in amazement. "I know he didn't take the charm."

"Mrs. Howard telephoned to him," Ned explained. "I suppose she meant well, but Basha thought he had been accused of the theft. He intends to run away before he is arrested."

"We must stop him, Ned."

"You're the only one who can explain to Basha, Nancy. That's why I came for you."

"I'll be ready in an instant."

She ran back into the house for her hat, and bidding a hasty good-bye to Mrs. Howard and

the girls, rejoined Ned. The couple drove
swiftly to Basha's rooming place, only to be
informed that the youth had departed.

"Which way did he go?" Ned demanded.

"Down Fulton Street toward the railway
station."

They resumed the pursuit, and a few blocks
farther on were gratified to glimpse the Hindu
student trudging along with his heavy suitcase.
Ned halted the car at the curbing.

"I didn't steal the charm!" Basha cried,
before either he or Nancy could speak a word.
"Let me go in peace, I beg of you!"

"We don't want you to go, Basha," Nancy
assured him kindly. "It's all a mistake."

"You have found the charm?"

"No, but Mrs. Howard didn't mean to accuse
you of taking it. We all know you are innocent. There is no need for you to run away."

A tear trickled down Basha's cheek, and
when he tried to express his gratitude words
failed him.

"You are very good," he murmured at last.
"Very kind. I will do all I am able to help
you recover the charm, for now that it is gone
your good luck will end."

"I am not so sure of that," Nancy replied.
"I've always been considered a lucky person,
even before Rai gave me the charm."

"Rai?" Basha inquired sharply.

"Yes. Do you know him?"

"Only casually. I have met him a few times. Last evening he telephoned me."

Ned and Nancy exchanged significant glances. Here, they thought, was an unexpected clue.

"Was this after the dance?" Nancy asked.

"Yes, he telephoned me at my rooming house."

"And by any chance did you mention my name?"

Basha was surprised at the question. "Yes, I did," he admitted. "I told him of your wonderful personality."

"And my ivory charm?" Nancy prompted.

"I did mention it, I believe."

"I think that explains everything," Nancy said quietly to Ned. "My bedroom at the fraternity house is on the first floor and I slept soundly."

"I did not mean to reveal anything of importance," Basha said in alarm. "What have I done?"

"It isn't your fault," Nancy assured him kindly. "However, I am afraid Rai has my charm. Tell me, where is the man now?"

"I have no idea. He telephoned from a hotel and mentioned that he was leaving the city in an hour."

"Don't look so glum, Basha," Ned said. "No one blames you. Jump in the car and we'll take you home."

Enroute to the rooming house, the Hindu

student assured Nancy over and over that he was heartsick at the outcome of the casual telephone call. He seemed especially downcast because he firmly believed that the girl's good fortune would desert her.

"Don't take the matter too seriously," Nancy urged him as they parted. "I have faith I'll recover the charm."

During the long ride back to River Heights, some time later that day, neither she nor Ned talked a great deal. They both felt discouraged and blue.

"I guess the party was a flop after all," Ned said as Nancy alighted at her own door.

"No, it wasn't. I had a wonderful time."

"But you lost your charm."

"I'll recover it again. My first move will be to trace Rai."

However, two days elapsed during which no word was heard of either Rai or the missing Coya. Mr. Drew had devoted many hours to the case, only to be confronted with defeat at every turn.

"Rai must have a secret hide-out," he told Nancy. "Otherwise, we'd surely locate him."

"At least we're still in touch with Miss Allison," Nancy returned, "and I have the incriminating documents which will convict her. And this is the day of my appointment, you know."

"You must be very careful what you do or

say," the lawyer cautioned. "I fear you are getting into deep water."

"Not so deep that I can't manage to swim out," Nancy smiled confidently.

A few hours later, enroute to the Stackpole residence, she did not feel quite so courageous. She knew that Coya's future as well as her own safety might depend upon the outcome of her meeting with Anita Allison. Would she prove a match for the clever woman?

"My only chance is to work upon her weakness for mysticism," Nancy thought. "I must play a part—and that part will require all my skill and cunning."

CHAPTER XX

A Hypnotic Trance

Nancy was escorted into Doctor Stackpole's private study, where she found him nervously pacing the floor.

"Ah! I am glad that you have arrived early," he said in relief to Nancy. "To tell you the truth, I am beginning to wonder if we have made a wise move in inviting Miss Allison here."

"In what way do you mean?"

"Something may go wrong. Then serious consequences may result if we have made a mistake."

"There can be no mistake, Doctor Stackpole. The documents in our possession conclusively prove her guilt."

"Yes, that is so. But if Miss Allison suspects that her true character has been exposed, she may resort to violence. I am afraid for your sake, Miss Drew."

"I'll be on my guard," promised Nancy. "Just show me where I am to hide."

Unwillingly the elderly man indicated an alcove just off the study which served as a tiny

conservatory. It was filled with palms and potted plants, offering an excellent hiding place where Nancy could hear and see everything without herself being visible. She chose a nook behind a large pottery vase.

Scarcely had she secreted herself when the doorbell rang. Doctor Stackpole hurried to answer it. He was utterly unprepared for the sight which greeted his eyes. Miss Allison, wearing a long flowing white costume and turban, with a jewel-bound book in her hand, entered the room as one walking in a trance.

"This way," the professor stammered, moving toward the library.

He offered Miss Allison a chair which she ignored. She stared at her host with a glazed expression in her eyes.

"You are interested in mysticism?" she murmured, before the dazed teacher could speak. "We are, I believe, of one spirit in this matter. I shall read, that we may find communion together."

With one arm outstretched in a grandiloquent gesture, she began to read from the jeweled volume. Nancy knew by the blank expression on Doctor Stackpole's face that the poor man was too stunned by the exhibition to comprehend a word, but by the time Miss Allison had finished the passage he had recovered his usual poise.

"A beautiful quotation, Miss Allison," he

said. "But our time is short and we must talk of India."

"Ah, yes," the woman sighed. "India—the land of adventure and mystery. What tales I could tell of its glamorous rulers!"

"Perhaps you could tell me of Iama Togara," Doctor Stackpole suggested cautiously. "I fear that the stories which filter to us in the west are but half-truths."

"The real story of how Iama Togara became a great ruler has never been told," Miss Allison boasted. "You would not believe me were I to say that I aided in placing him on the throne."

"Indeed I would," Doctor Stackpole answered quietly.

"The untimely death of the heir-apparent, a youth named Coya, left the affairs of the province in a hopeless muddle," Miss Allison explained sadly, dabbing at her eyes with a handkerchief. "I was deeply grieved over his demise."

"I can imagine you were!" Nancy thought scornfully. "It's easy to see your tender heart is broken!"

"The province was plunged into turmoil," Miss Allison continued. "I knew that a good ruler would have to be found quickly if war were to be avoided. I decided to act—you understand that I was motivated entirely by my desire to aid the poor natives."

"Oh, certainly, certainly," Doctor Stackpole murmured, endeavoring to hide his contempt for the woman.

"Through various political and psychic connections I was able to place Iama Togara on the throne."

"And your reward?" Doctor Stackpole inquired.

For the first time Miss Allison regarded him with a slight trace of suspicion.

"Nothing," she answered shortly. "I did it because of my feeling for India."

Doctor Stackpole attempted to encourage Miss Allison to reveal more, but as it became apparent that she was regarding his interest with distrust, he switched to another subject, speaking of a certain type of carved Indian vase which had intrigued him.

"I have tried to buy such a vase at various art stores," he remarked, "but I have been unable to locate one which pleases me."

Miss Allison nodded understandingly. "I know exactly the sort of work you mean, and it is difficult to secure. However, I have a friend, an Indian, who might be able to find the vase for you."

"You are very kind. I don't suppose your friend by any chance could be a circus man named Rai?"

Again Miss Allison regarded the professor suspiciously.

"Certainly not," she replied stiffly. "I have never heard of such a person."

By this time it was evident to Nancy that Miss Allison was entirely too wary to say anything which might involve her in the scheme to deprive Coya of his rightful inheritance. If the woman were to be compelled to confess, more drastic methods would have to be employed.

Quietly Nancy slipped from her hiding place, left the house by a side exit and walked around to the front door, where she rapped. A maid promptly admitted her and escorted her to the library.

Immediately the Drew girl began to act a part. She pretended to be greatly surprised to find Miss Allison at the teacher's home and apologized for intruding.

"We were just having a pleasant little chat about India," Doctor Stackpole said. "Miss Allison is considered an authority upon the subject of mysticism."

"How interesting!" Nancy exclaimed. "I have always been deeply intrigued by that subject myself. In fact, some of my friends believe that I have psychic powers."

"Indeed," Miss Allison remarked disparagingly.

"Yes," Nancy continued glibly, "I have always felt that I was endowed with the ability to look back into the past. Under correct

conditions, I have faith that I could demonstrate this strange power.''

''Psychic powers are far more rare than you think,'' Miss Allison said unpleasantly.

''Nevertheless, I am certain I have this ability. If you wish, I will prove it.''

The woman hesitated, and then before she could speak, Doctor Stackpole said quickly:

''By all means, Miss Drew. Such a demonstration should prove interesting.''

''Lower the blinds,'' Nancy commanded.

When the room was shrouded in semi-darkness, she said to Miss Allison:

''I must have your turban.''

''This is nonsense,'' the woman complained as she unwillingly gave up the head-gear.

Placing herself in front of a dark velvet drapery, Nancy closed her eyes. She began to rock slowly back and forth, chanting in low, musical tones. At first her words were unintelligible. Then she began quoting passages from the documents which she had taken from Peter Putnam.

Miss Allison leaned forward, gripping the arms of her chair. Her eyes dilated with fear. She tried to speak, but made only a choking noise in her throat.

Nancy knew that it was time for the climax of her act. She took a step toward the woman, and her hand swept outward in a gesture of accusation.

"YOU are the guilty person!" she proclaimed. "You are the person who deprived Coya of his right to the throne and brought him to this country. Confess! Confess!"

For an instant Miss Allison seemed too stunned to move. Then she dropped down upon her knees before Nancy, sobbing wildly.

"Yes, yes! I did it! I employed Rai to kidnap the boy that Iama Togara might be put upon the throne! I did it for India."

"You kidnaped Coya because your reward was a precious treasure," Nancy corrected sternly.

Before Miss Allison could make a response to this accusation, there came an unfortunate interruption. A telephone rang in the adjoining room.

Miss Allison straightened. The look of fear left her face and she became more composed.

"I must answer," Doctor Stackpole murmured as the instrument continued to ring.

Realizing that the spell was broken, Nancy expediently emerged from her "trance." She had secured the confession which she sought. The professor would serve as a reliable witness against Miss Allison when the proper time should come.

"Well, did my psychic demonstration convince you?" Nancy smiled.

"It did. I—I don't suppose you remember much of what you said?"

Nancy was not compelled to reply, for Doctor Stackpole appeared in the doorway just then.

"The call is for you, Miss Drew. Your father wishes to speak with you."

Nancy hastened to the telephone. "What is it, Dad?" she asked hurriedly.

"I really shouldn't have bothered you," the lawyer apologized. "I merely telephoned to learn if you are safe. Since you left I've been worried."

"I'm all right, Dad. Everything is going along splendidly. Only I can't take time to tell you about it now. I'll call you back in a few minutes."

Nancy hung up the receiver and returned to the library. She paused in the doorway to stare in horror. Doctor Stackpole lay stretched out on the floor, unconscious. His head was bleeding from a deep wound caused by a heavy blow from a book-end. Miss Allison had disappeared.

"That woman did this!" Nancy thought as she went over to the professor's side. "She struck him with the book-end because she was afraid he would reveal what he had heard!"

While Nancy was trying vainly to raise the man to a sitting posture, the front doorbell rang. Instead of going to answer it the girl called loudly for help.

"Coming!" a masculine voice shouted.

The next moment Ned Nickerson ran into the

room, only to stop short as he beheld the professor lying on the floor.

"Doctor Stackpole is badly hurt," Nancy cried frantically. "At his age such a blow may prove fatal. We must act quickly to save him!"

CHAPTER XXI

The True Rajah

Ned and Nancy worked silently over the aged teacher, and were relieved to notice that his heart-beat seemed regular, although weak.

"He'll be all right in a few minutes, I think," Ned said after a time. "But we need ice or a cold water bottle."

"I'll see if I can't find something."

Nancy hastened to the kitchen. Both the cook and the maid had vanished, but the refrigerator tray offered an ample supply of ice cubes. Nancy was searching for a bag in which to put them when she heard a slight noise in the pantry. It sounded as if a window had opened.

Tiptoeing to the door, she peered into the adjoining room. A boy in tattered, grimy garments was stealthily climbing through the window.

"He probably means to steal something from the pantry," Nancy thought.

As she had expected, the boy reached up on a shelf and took down a freshly baked pie. He did not bother to cut himself a piece but greedily dipped in with his fingers.

180

Nancy opened the pantry door. The boy, terrified, whirled about to face her.

"Coya!" she cried.

The Indian lad laughed in relief and joy.

"Coya escape from Rai and run away," he announced, grinning broadly. "Two days and nights without food make me very hungry. Pie look very good."

"Eat it all," Nancy urged. "I'm sure Doctor Stackpole won't begrudge it to you. But why did you come here? Why didn't you return to our house?"

"Coya afraid Rai look there for him. Rai somewhere here in city now. He trail me like dog."

"Then you were wise to come here," Nancy acknowledged. "But a few minutes ago Doctor Stackpole was hurt."

While she was explaining what had occurred, Ned appeared in the kitchen doorway. He had come to find out what had detained Nancy and was greatly startled upon encountering Coya. However, with the professor in such urgent need of attention, there was no time to hear the Hindu lad's story of his escape from Rai.

"Doctor Stackpole is conscious now," Ned told Nancy anxiously. "But I need the ice."

They returned with it together, and after ministering to the elderly tutor were able to lift him to a couch. After a time the man's strength came back and he gazed about the

room, trying to localize objects and persons. Coya had followed Nancy and Ned to the library and stood gazing sorrowfully at his stricken teacher.

"Is it really you—Coya?" the professor murmured.

"Yes, yes," the lad said eagerly. "It is Coya. I mean—it is I," he stammered, trying to use the English which had been taught him.

"I shall always be proud that I served as your tutor," Doctor Stackpole said in a half whisper. "The lost Rajah!"

Coya stared in bewilderment at Nancy as if expecting her to offer an explanation for the man's strange words.

"It is true," the girl told him gravely. "We have evidence which proves that you were kidnaped from your own country by persons who placed Iama Togara on the throne in your stead."

For a long moment Coya did not speak. But tears of joy trickled down his brown cheeks as he eyed Nancy with a worshipful gaze.

"Always have I known in my heart that I was born to rule," he said quietly. "But without your help I could never have done it."

"Although you have a clear claim to the throne, it may not be easy to make your countrymen acknowledge you as their ruler," Nancy warned. "Your campaign must be carefully planned. Until the hour arrives when

you will assume your rightful place, you must forget that you are a rajah.''

The boy nodded gravely. ''Coya knows many men may try to kill him.''

Doctor Stackpole slowly arose from the couch.

''If you will excuse me, I shall retire to my room now. My head aches severely.''

''Shan't we call a physician?'' Nancy inquired anxiously.

''No, no, I shall be quite myself after I have slept.'' The man moved towards the door and then paused. ''Coya must remain with me until Rai and Miss Allison are apprehended. He will be safer here than elsewhere.''

''I doubt that they would ever think of searching at this house for him,'' Nancy admitted.

''I shall have Coya's room prepared at once,'' Doctor Stackpole said. He bowed to both Nancy and Ned. ''You must forgive me for deserting you in this manner. I am not myself.''

After the tutor had retired, Nancy and Ned explained to Coya the details of Miss Allison's plot against him. The boy in turn told them of Rai's cruelty during the past few days of captivity.

''Rai kept me in a small room and when he went away even for an hour, bound me fast to a chair. I did not have enough to eat.

Every night he beat me. Yesterday I managed to untie the ropes and ran away.''

''You have had a very bitter experience,'' Nancy said sympathetically. ''But you will be safe now that you are here with Doctor Stackpole.''

''Coya stay very close in house,'' the boy smiled. ''Never go outside again until Rai is captured.''

Nancy arose to depart. It occurred to her to ask the lad if during his period of captivity he had observed Rai wearing the missing ivory charm. The boy's response was in the negative.

''I'd give a great deal to recover that lucky piece,'' Nancy remarked. ''Somehow I can't help feeling that it guards a strange secret.''

''Rai often hint same thing,'' Coya said gravely. ''Once he say charm have power of life or death.''

''That was a queer remark,'' Nancy mused. ''I wonder——''

She left the thought unexpressed, and after bidding Coya good-bye, departed with Ned.

''What were you about to say in regard to the charm?'' Ned asked curiously as they drove away.

''Oh, nothing,'' Nancy responded carelessly. ''I was just speculating.''

During the remainder of the ride she was unusually quiet. Ned knew full well that she

was working out some theory, but he did not urge her to reveal it.

Nancy slept a little later than usual the next morning and had just finished dressing, when Hannah called up the stairway that she was wanted on the telephone.

"I think it is Doctor Stackpole," the housekeeper said. "He seems greatly excited."

"I have distressing news for you, Miss Drew," the professor told her in a strained, tense voice. "During the night Coya was kidnaped from my home."

"Kidnaped!" Nancy echoed. "It can't be!"

"I blame myself, Miss Drew. I should have watched the boy. But I had no idea that Rai was in the neighborhood. This morning the maid told me that she saw a man answering his description prowling about the house. Apparently, when the opportunity came, he entered and took Coya."

"This is dreadful," Nancy cried. "I fear for the boy's life."

"Yes, we must act quickly if we are to save him. But what can we do?"

"I'll talk to my father," Nancy said. "He may have a plan."

She hung up the receiver and hastened to the dining room where Mr. Drew was eating his breakfast. In terse sentences she revealed what had occurred.

"The case calls for drastic action," the

lawyer responded grimly. "You are right in saying that unless Rai is apprehended immediately Coya's life will be the forfeit."

"Shall we notify the police?"

"We'll do more than that. We leave for Washington, D. C. on the eleven o'clock plane."

"Washington?" Nancy gasped.

"Yes, we'll tell our story to my friend, Mr. George, whose offices are there. Whenever I have an international problem come up in my cases, I turn to him for aid. He's the very person to take care of this situation. How soon can you be ready to start, Nancy?"

"In fifteen minutes, if necessary."

"Good! I must attend to some business at the office now, but I'll be back here for you in an hour."

Crumpling his napkin, Mr. Drew arose from the table and walked from the dining room. Hannah and Nancy stood staring blankly after him, still dazed by the rapidity with which he had made the important decision. Nancy was the first to recover.

"Come, Hannah," she directed. "There is no time to lose if Dad and I are to make the plane. You must help me pack."

CHAPTER XXII

The Woman on the Bridge

Eleven o'clock found Nancy and her father at the River Heights airport boarding the regular transport for Washington, D. C. A few hours later, after a pleasant but uneventful journey, they arrived at their destination.

Carson Drew had wired ahead for an appointment with his friend, Mr. George. A special car had been dispatched to the air field to meet the lawyer and his daughter, and they were escorted directly to the offices of the man who was to aid them. There they told their story, and were deeply gratified when they were promised that no stone should be left unturned in the search for Coya and his abductors.

"The aid of both United States and British government officials as well as private detectives will be enlisted," Nancy and her father were assured. "If Coya is still alive he will be found."

Within the hour a reward of five thousand dollars had been posted for the return of the boy or for information leading to the arrest of his kidnapers. Nancy was able to furnish an

excellent description of both Rai and Miss Allison, and a photograph of the latter was located in the government files.

"It's my opinion that Coya will be found in the vicinity of River Heights," was Nancy's decision, "but I'll be glad to stay here. It's interesting talking to big detectives."

"You may be right about the boy," Mr. Drew admitted. "However, the matter is out of our hands now. By seeing that government officials have been notified, we have done everything in our power. From now on we must play a waiting game."

"Waiting was never one of my really strong points," Nancy smiled. "I crave action."

"After all, it isn't reasonable to expect Coya to be found in twenty-four hours."

"Sometimes I wonder if he'll ever be seen again, Dad. Since my Ivory Charm was stolen things have turned out badly."

"You're not becoming superstitious, I hope, Nancy."

"No. Yet I can't help but feel that if I could recover my ivory piece Coya too might be found. It is so hard just to sit and wait and hope."

"There is one thing we can do," Mr. Drew said, moving toward the hotel telephone. "I'll send a wire to the River Heights bank warning the officials to deny Miss Allison access to her safety vault in the event that she should return to secure the treasure deposited in her name."

"Do you think she would dare to appear there?"

"I doubt it, Nancy, but we must close every loophole. I'll have a detective stationed constantly at the bank to be on the lookout for her."

Nancy and Mr. Drew had intended to return home the following day, but their plans underwent a swift change when the girl received an unexpected letter written on White House stationery. Nancy excitedly held the missive to the light before opening it, as if trying to divine what was contained in the envelope.

"Dad, do you suppose it's from the President?" she asked, half in banter.

"How should I know?" Mr. Drew replied with a smile. "Why not open it and end the suspense?"

Nancy unsealed the envelope and read the signature first. The letter had been written by the secretary to the President's wife, and was an invitation to attend a luncheon at the White House the following afternoon. The note mentioned that one of the official limousines would call for the guest at her hotel at the appointed hour.

"Such an invitation is practically mandatory," Mr. Drew declared, "so we'll cancel our Pullman reservations and stay over another day. It's not often that one has an opportunity to lunch with the wife of the President."

"How did it happen that I am invited?" asked Nancy.

"I presume through Mr. George," her father replied.

When the excited girl reached the White House, she was graciously received. The distinguished first lady told Nancy that Mr. George had spoken of her work as an amateur detective, and she asked many questions about the girl's famous cases. She introduced her to a small group of personal friends who had gathered to do honor in an informal way to the celebrated young detective.

An hour later Nancy stepped from the White House limousine at her hotel door and hurriedly entered the elevator. She burst into the Drew apartment only to find her father pacing restlessly up and down, a worried expression on his face.

"Why, what is wrong, Dad?" she asked.

"The Department of Justice has been ringing the phone at fifteen-minute intervals ever since you left, Nancy. They are holding a suspect they think is Miss Allison, and want you to identify her."

"Where did they capture her?" Nancy inquired eagerly.

"Here in Washington."

"Then I can tell them the woman is not Miss Allison," Nancy said with positive conviction. "She would never come here, I am sure. I sus-

pect she is not far from River Heights at this very moment."

"You may be right," Mr. Drew agreed. "But it would be better to go with them as they wish."

Mr. Drew called the Department and in an incredibly short time an operative whisked them away in a government car. Presently the automobile stopped at an old stone building at the door of which a detective stood guard. He conducted the little party into an upper room and brought Nancy face to face with a woman who bore a striking resemblance to Miss Allison, but who was merely the victim of that unfortunate fact. After Nancy had absolved her the woman asked curiously:

"Aren't you Miss Drew?"

"Well, that identification is correct anyhow," Nancy responded, casting a mischievous glance at the government men.

She returned with her father to the hotel, but before the day was ended they were called upon to identify a second suspect. It was another useless trip, and Nancy convinced her father that they could do nothing more in Washington. Accordingly they took a fast night train for River Heights.

Word soon spread that the Drews were home, and many visitors called at the residence to hear the details of Nancy's exciting experience. She answered all questions politely, yet be-

grudged the time required to entertain uninvited guests.

"The story of Coya's kidnaping has become public property somehow. I am afraid many people think more of re-telling the details than they do of trying to help," she complained to her father.

Each day Nancy made a point of visiting the local police station to inquire what progress, if any, had been made in the case. At the River Heights bank she was told that Miss Allison had not called for the treasure deposited in her name. Many clues developed, but all proved false.

Early one evening, as Nancy was walking slowly home from her father's office, she was feeling unusually blue and discouraged. For the first time she was very nearly ready to acknowledge defeat. She feared that Coya would never be found.

In a reflective mood the girl strolled in the direction of a little used river bridge, a favorite place for her when she wanted to think out problems. She found a strange companionship in the swirling, black waters as they rushed past the great pillars many feet below her.

As Nancy approached the bridge, she was relieved to find that the foot-path was deserted. She would be alone as she wished. Suddenly she paused, startled.

Not twenty feet away there loomed up the

figure of a woman. She wore a white turban, and the wind whipped her flowing robes about her crazily. As Nancy watched, the strange person approached the bridge railing. She stood there as one transfixed, gazing down intently into the angry waters.

"I believe that's Miss Allison!" Nancy thought tensely.

CHAPTER XXIII

A Leap into the Dark

Softly Nancy stole forward, taking care to make no sound. Unaware that anyone was approaching, the woman stood motionless, gazing moodily down into the stream which swirled beneath the bridge. Then she turned slightly so that the light from a street lamp flickered across her face.

"It *is* Miss Allison," Nancy confirmed her identification.

She was tempted to accost the fugitive, but wisely considered that she might be no physical match for the woman. At such an hour few pedestrians crossed this bridge.

"I must telephone for the authorities," she reasoned.

Stealing quietly away, Nancy ran to the nearest drug store.

"May I use your phone?" she asked.

"Sure, go ahead," the clerk replied.

Calling the local authorities, Nancy tersely revealed her information and was assured that men would be dispatched immediately.

"Approach the place quietly," she warned

the police. "Otherwise, Miss Allison may be alarmed and try to escape."

After completing the call Nancy hastened back to the bridge. During her absence Miss Allison had not moved. Greatly relieved, Nancy secreted herself in a clump of bushes near by to wait for the police.

The minutes dragged slowly by. Nancy grew worried and impatient. Why did the authorities delay? Would they never come?

Then she heard the muffled roar of a motor. She felt certain it must be the police car, for it stopped some distance from the bridge. Miss Allison had caught the faint hum of the running engine and Nancy saw her glance about alertly. Officers were moving stealthily along the footpath now. The woman identified them instantly and realized why they were approaching. She turned as if to flee in the opposite direction. Nancy emerged from her hiding place to block the way.

Miss Allison knew that she was trapped. She wheeled, and before anyone divined her intention, climbed the high rail of the bridge.

"Stop! Stop!" Nancy screamed.

Miss Allison poised on the rail for an instant; then, with a fearful cry, she plunged down into the river. Nancy darted to the railing. She could see the woman struggling frantically in the water. The current was carrying her swiftly down-stream.

Jerking off coat and shoes, the girl mounted the railing and dived. She struck the water cleanly, and after boring straight downward for a few feet emerged upon the surface. Shaking the water from her eyes, she looked around her and saw that Miss Allison was still struggling, although the thrashing of her arms was rapidly growing weaker.

A dozen powerful strokes brought Nancy to the woman's side. Approaching from the rear, she sought to grip her in a safe cross-chest carry. Miss Allison fought feebly to elude her rescuer.

"Let me drown! Let me drown!" she pleaded.

Nancy's only reaction was to tighten her hold under the woman's armpit. Miss Allison twisted and turned and tried to climb on the girl's shoulders. The struggle was an exhausting one for them both, and by the time the woman became submissive Nancy was worn and gasping for breath.

The swift current had carried the pair far down-stream. For a minute Nancy allowed herself to drift with it as she recaptured her wind. Then, with her free right arm she struck out again and soon reached shallow water, just as two policemen rowed up in a boat which they had found not far from the bridge. They relieved the rescuer of her charge and escorted Miss Allison to the police car under guard.

"We'll need you along to offer evidence,"

one of the men told Nancy. "You can get some dry clothes from the matron at the station."

Half an hour later, when Nancy viewed Miss Allison in the chief's office, it seemed to her that the woman's entire attitude had changed. As the girl began to question her this became more apparent. Miss Allison had lost her former arrogance; her spirit was crushed and broken.

"I am sorry—about everything," she mumbled. "I don't know what made me do it."

"Then tell us what has been done with Coya," Nancy urged. "Where has Rai taken him?"

"It will go easier for you if you tell everything," the chief suggested quietly.

"Coya has been hidden at the abandoned house," Miss Allison admitted reluctantly. "Rai and Jasper Batt guard him there."

Nancy did not wait to learn more, for she feared that Coya might have been harmed by his captors and require medical aid. Every moment was precious.

With a picked group of policemen she drove directly to the burned house. The officers searched the premises thoroughly.

"There is no one here," they reported to Nancy, who waited.

"You searched the tunnel?"

"Yes, it is empty. Miss Allison evidently lied."

Sick with disappointment, Nancy was forced

to return home while the policemen went back to the station to report their failure. Carson Drew met his daughter at the door and heard her vivid account of the evening's adventure.

"You did splendid work in capturing that woman," he praised. "But I shudder when I think that she might have drowned you."

"My life-saving course stood me in good stead," Nancy returned. "If I hadn't known that I could battle the current, I'd never have attempted the rescue."

"I'm not so sure of that," Mr. Drew replied severely. "I rather think you would have taken the risk anyway."

"I was bitterly disappointed, Dad, that we failed to find Coya. I was so certain Miss Allison was telling the truth."

"Perhaps Rai moved the boy to another hiding place without informing Miss Allison."

"That's possible," Nancy agreed. "In the morning I believe I'll run out to the house and look over the place myself. I may stumble on a clue."

She was abroad the next morning before breakfast, and her first act was to telephone George Fayne.

"What's the idea of getting me out of bed so early?" the latter demanded crossly as she recognized her chum's voice at the other end of the wire.

"I can't tell you now," Nancy answered,

"but if you're in the mood for an adventure be waiting on your doorstep in half an hour."

"I'll be waiting," George promised, now thoroughly awakened.

A little later the two girls were speeding swiftly toward the Allison property. Enroute Nancy explained everything that had happened during the night.

"I've been thinking it over and can't help but believe that Miss Allison told the truth last night," Nancy said. "Or at least she feels sure that Coya is hidden at the old house. Now it occurs to me that the police may have missed the branch-off of the tunnel when they made their search. That's why I'm going back there this morning."

Approaching the Allison property, Nancy secreted the car in a clump of trees and the girls walked the remaining distance. They were moving along the well-worn path when George caught her chum's hand.

"Someone is coming!" she whispered.

They dodged back into the bushes just as Jasper Batt strode into view. He carried a small package in his hand and a thermos bottle could be seen protruding from a coat pocket. The girls waited until he had disappeared before they emerged from their hiding place.

"Mr. Batt is taking a lunch to someone—or rather a breakfast," Nancy amended. "Let's follow. He may lead us to Coya and Rai!"

As they cautiously trailed the old watchman, it became evident that he was heading for the door in the rock. They saw the man pause by the cliff.

"How does he intend to enter?" Nancy speculated. "Watch closely."

They saw the watchman take a heavy stick and rap six times in succession on the rock door. He waited several minutes, then repeated the taps.

The girls heard a faint click. Jasper Batt stepped back a pace, waiting expectantly. The massive door slowly swung outward.

CHAPTER XXIV

Prisoners

When the door had opened wide, Jasper Batt thrust the package of food and the thermos bottle into the tunnel. Nancy and George heard him speak a few words to someone inside, but the girls were too far away to distinguish what was being said. After a moment the watchman firmly closed the rock door, and after making certain that it was locked, walked swiftly off into the woods.

"He brought some food to a prisoner in the tunnel," George whispered in awe.

"It must be Coya," Nancy added. "I'll soon find out!"

"What do you intend to do?" George questioned fearfully as her chum moved forward.

"I'm going to try Jasper Batt's trick of opening the door."

Selecting a heavy stick, Nancy rapped sharply on the rock, six times in rapid succession. She waited expectantly, but nothing happened.

"Batt repeated the signals twice," George reminded her.

"So he did. I'll try that."

201

Again Nancy knocked on the door. This time the girls heard the familiar click which told them that a latch had been unfastened. They moved back, making room for the heavy barrier to swing outward.

"It's opening!" George observed fearfully. "Please don't go inside, Nancy."

The girls peered into the dark interior of the tunnel, but at first could see nothing.

"Coya! Coya!" Nancy called.

"Help! Help!" a feeble voice responded.

Nancy and George exchanged startled glances. They knew that it was not the Indian lad who had answered. The voice sounded familiar, yet they could not place it.

"Who is it?" Nancy shouted.

"Putnam—Peter Putnam! That fiend, Batt, has me chained to a post! Come and help me!"

"It may be a trap," George whispered nervously.

Nancy shook her head. By this time her eyes had grown accustomed to the dark cavern and she could dimly make out a figure chained to an object not far from the entrance. Boldly she entered the tunnel, and after a moment's hesitation George followed her.

"Thank the fates you've come in time!" Putnam murmured brokenly as the girls reached him. "Those villains meant that I should die in this dark, filthy hole. Dead men tell no tales."

"And have you a tale to tell?" Nancy asked alertly.

Peter Putnam rattled his chains angrily. "Get me out of here and don't do so much talking! Unfasten my fetters."

"I'll be very glad to accommodate you, Mr. Putnam, but not until you have revealed where Rai has hidden Coya."

"Why should I tell you anything?" the prisoner growled. "You're the girl who stole my papers from the coffee pot! Oh, you thought I wouldn't find out that you had substituted another piece of paper, but I noticed it right away."

"The papers weren't yours," Nancy said. "Right now it's to your interest to tell me everything you know about Rai and Coya. Unless you do, I fear I shall be compelled to leave you here."

"It was your fault that I got into this predicament," Putnam retorted bitterly. "If it hadn't been for those papers——"

"You should never have stolen them from Batt," Nancy replied severely. "But that's neither here nor there. If you prefer not to talk, then we'll leave."

Although she had no intention of abandoning the man to his fate, Nancy turned as if to depart. As she had expected, the move brought Putnam to his senses.

"All right, I'll tell you everything I know,"

he gave in. "Unfasten the chains at once."

"I prefer to hear your story first," Nancy said evenly.

She knew that Putnam, once released, could never be trusted to keep his agreement.

"What do you want to know?"

"Tell me where Coya has been hidden."

"Rai has him at my place—a prisoner in the loft. I was to get a tidy sum for keeping my mouth shut about it. But this is the pay I get! Chained to a post!"

"You are telling the truth?" Nancy demanded sharply.

"If you don't believe me I'll take you there and prove it!"

"That's exactly what I want you to do! Now just be patient and we'll release you as quickly as we can."

Nancy and George set to work, and after nearly half an hour of discouraging labor managed to break the lock of the chain with a huge rock. Putnam crept to the tunnel entrance, whimpering from pain as circulation returned to his cramped limbs.

"You'll be all right in a few minutes," Nancy encouraged him. "Here, lean on my shoulder and I'll help you to the car."

"What will you do when you get to my place?" Putnam asked a little later as the girls drove away from the Allison property.

"I haven't decided yet," Nancy answered.

"That fellow Rai is a fox. You'll be no match for him."

"You must help us, Mr. Putnam."

. The man made no response and Nancy, casting a quick glance in his direction, correctly read the expression on his face. Peter Putnam would look after himself and had no intention of aiding any other person, be it friend or foe.

Presently Nancy drew near the miser's barn-like home and halted the car. She did not wish the running motor to warn Rai that anyone was approaching.

"You can sneak up to the house the back way," Putnam suggested, indicating a path which led through the underbrush. "I'll wait here."

Nancy and George regarded the miser with ill-concealed contempt; yet they made no protest at his decision, for they realized that his cowardice would prevent him from being of any real aid to them. Accordingly they crept toward the house alone.

Unknown to them, Rai, in the loft of the barn, had caught a glimpse of the automobile coming down the road. He smiled wickedly as he watched the girls steal cautiously toward the house.

"Rai will be ready for them!" he chuckled, descending the ladder to the lower floor. Then he stationed himself near the door and waited.

A few minutes later, after circling the house,

Nancy and George quietly twisted the knob and pushed the door open a tiny crack.

"The coast is clear, I think," Nancy whispered. "I can't hear a sound."

She opened the door wider and they entered on tiptoe. A harsh laugh caused them to wheel about. Rai slammed the door shut and faced them gloatingly.

"So! I now have two fair prisoners to enclose in my little cage!"

With one accord Nancy and George sprang at the man, hoping to overpower him and regain their freedom. Although they fought violently, Rai laughed aloud at their efforts. Without exerting himself unduly he held them off, and then, tiring of the cat and mouse game, caught up a piece of rope from the kitchen table and trussed them securely.

Dazed and frightened, the girls eyed Rai silently, wondering what punishment he would inflict upon them. In all their experience they had never encountered a man with such strength.

"What have you done with Coya?" Nancy gasped, recovering her poise.

"Ah! So that is why you came? Coya is dead."

"I do not believe it," Nancy cried. "You have him hidden in the loft."

As if to confirm her words, the girls heard a slight noise overhead. Rai smiled blandly.

"You are correct. Coya lives, but his hours

are numbered. He must die that Iama Togara
may rule in peace.''

''You can't realize what you are saying, Rai,''
Nancy said pleadingly. ''The boy has never
done you any harm. Let him go free.''

''No, it is decreed that Coya must die by my
hand. He shall die slowly and in a manner be-
fitting a rajah.''

Turning his back upon the two girls, Rai
moved toward the ladder which led to the loft.

CHAPTER XXV

The Secret of the Charm

"Wait!" Nancy cried frantically. "Rai, you must be out of your mind even to think of such a horrible deed. Don't you realize that if you harm Coya the authorities will punish you?"

The Hindu paused, his foot on the lower rung of the ladder.

"Rai is safe from all harm," he returned gravely. "The wonderful Ivory Charm bestows absolute protection."

"So it was you who stole the lucky piece from my bedroom! I suspected it."

Rai laughed gloatingly as he significantly tapped his breast to indicate that he wore the charm hidden beneath his shirt.

"Never will I give it away again, for not only does my charm bring good luck to the wearer but it has the power of life and death!"

"What do you mean by that, Rai?"

Again the man laughed softly. "There are many mysteries which may never be revealed."

"You are hopelessly superstitious if you believe the charm will protect you from the

police,'' Nancy said, sparring for time. ''Miss Allison already has been arrested.''

She knew from Rai's change of expression that he had not heard this piece of news before. However, he merely said suavely:

''My duty does not change. Coya must die.''

In vain did both Nancy and George plead with Rai, but he paid no heed to their words. He mounted the ladder and vanished into the loft.

''We must do something!'' Nancy said desperately, tugging at her ropes. ''We can't let Rai commit this dreadful crime!''

Both girls worked at their bonds until their wrists were cut and bleeding. It was impossible to loosen the ropes.

Overhead, Nancy and George could hear Rai muttering in a sing-song voice, apparently saying a weird incantation over Coya. They could distinguish moans from the boy, and knew that he must be suffering intensely. Then all became quiet.

''Ah!'' they heard Rai murmur in triumph, ''Coya enters the eternal sleep from which there is no awakening. Only the Ivory Charm can save him now—and I have it.''

''Did you hear what he said?'' Nancy whispered to George. ''The Charm! If only we could get it, we still might save poor Coya!''

''How can anything save him now?'' George asked hopelessly.

"The charm would bring him back to consciousness," Nancy said, thinking aloud. "I am sure of it. For a long while I have suspected the truth—now I am certain of it. The Ivory Charm guards the secret of life and death!"

"Do you realize what you are saying?" George gasped.

"Yes! It all comes back to me now—what Doctor Stackpole told me about the life-giving fluid sometimes found in the hidden cavities of ancient Indian charms!"

"Nancy, I don't know what you mean."

"We must try to get that piece, George. It is our only hope of saving Coya."

"We'll never untie these knots. It's useless to try."

Nancy would not give up so easily. She strained and tugged until she was exhausted. Tears of disappointment came into her eyes. She tried not to think of poor Coya in the loft above.

"Listen!" George whispered tensely.

"A car in the lane! Perhaps Putnam has brought help!"

George commanded a view of the window, and a moment later whispered excitedly that she could see several men stealing toward the house.

"They look like detectives, Nancy. Let's call for help."

"Wait until they are at the door," Nancy
cautioned. "Then all escape will be cut off for
Rai."

A minute later when the plainclothesmen
were near by, the girls raised their voices in
unison. Alarmed by their cries, Rai came
scrambling down from the loft just as the detectives flung open the door.

"Arrest that man!" Nancy cried, pointing
to Rai.

The man made a dive for the nearest window
but was caught roughly by the shoulder and
hauled back. Other detectives hastened to set
Nancy and George free.

"Coya is upstairs in the loft," the Drew girl
told the detectives as her ropes were being severed. "This fiend Rai tried to kill him. Even
now it may be too late!"

Several of the men rushed to the ladder while
Nancy remained for an instant to face Rai.

"Give me the Ivory Charm!" she commanded.

"It will do no good," Rai whined. "It will
not save Coya now."

"Give it to me!" Nancy repeated, and jerked
it from the cord about the man's neck.

She mounted the ladder to find the group of
dejected detectives standing in a semi-circle
about Coya, who lay stretched out on a blanket.
The lad's face was colorless and he did not appear to be breathing.

"We found the boy smothered beneath several heavy blankets," one of the men explained sadly. "I am afraid we have arrived too late. The boy is dead."

"Dead?" Nancy gasped. "Oh, that can't be!"

She dropped on one knee beside Coya and placed her ear against his thin chest. She could not hear the beating of his heart; yet it might be that the final spark of life had not been extinguished after all. The Ivory Charm offered the only hope.

Nancy still clutched the tiny elephant piece in her hand. She stared down at it in a puzzled way. If she should break off a tusk to explore the interior, she might lose the precious life-giving fluid should any be contained therein. But she felt that she must take the chance.

While the detectives watched in amazement, Nancy twisted off one of the elephant tusks. She uttered a little cry of triumph and relief. In the cavity of the elephant's body lay a tiny vial of fluid, light amber in color. Opening it, Nancy forced some of the liquid between Coya's lips. Then, with a prayer in her heart, she waited.

Minutes passed, and the color began to return to the boy's face. Soon he stirred slightly, and Nancy knew that now was the time to start artificial respiration.

With a sureness of method that surprised

even the detectives, she applied the emergency measures to the prostrate form. At the end of each exhalation she hoped that Coya would resume natural breathing. As the minutes elapsed and this did not occur, Nancy grew anxious. She feared that even with the aid of the magic potion the boy might not recover. Still she continued, never once varying the rhythm of the operation. At last, to her immense relief and joy, Coya began to breath naturally.

"The King will live!" she exclaimed exultingly. "Coya has been saved!"

As Nancy spoke these words the little brown boy opened his eyes and smiled at his benefactress for a fleeting moment. He was still too weak to speak.

"Coya owes his life and his future to you, Nancy," George, who was standing near by said softly. "By discovering the life-giving fluid you have solved the mystery of the Ivory Charm."

"Yes, but I am afraid I ruined the trinket by twisting off the elephant's tusk."

"The charm can be repaired," George replied. "But even if that is impossible, it has served its purpose."

In half an hour Coya had recovered sufficiently so that it was safe to move him to comfortable quarters. Nancy insisted that he be taken directly to her own home and established in the front bedroom.

"This chamber is scarcely elegant enough for a person of royal birth," she remarked laughingly to Hannah Gruen, "but I know it will seem very comfortable to Coya after all that he has been through."

"I blush with shame when I think that we allowed him to sleep in the garage room," the housekeeper returned self-accusingly.

"Coya didn't mind. It was far better than anything he had while he lived with Rai."

"I declare, I can't accustom myself to the idea that the boy is to inherit a throne," Mrs. Gruen said, shaking her head in a baffled way. "You're certain there's no mistake, Nancy?"

"Absolutely none. The documents I recovered give him an iron-clad claim. The British government will aid in deposing Iama Togara."

"It seems strange, having a rajah in the house," Mrs. Gruen continued in a tone of awe. "Should I address him as 'Your Highness?' "

"I imagine he would prefer to be called Coya, just as before," Nancy smiled.

Mr. Drew and the local authorities made every effort to keep the boy's identity a secret.

Rai and Miss Allison were given speedy trials, and after they both had confessed their guilt, were sentenced to long terms on an island prison. Jasper Batt, a willing tool of the pair, was confined to prison for a shorter period. Peter Putnam, although granted leniency by the court because he had aided in the capture of

Rai, was so severely censured by his neighbors that he abandoned his barn-like home and vanished from the state. The treasure deposited at the bank in Miss Allison's name was confiscated by the government and turned over to a guardian for Coya, from whose family it had been stolen.

Nancy received a pleasant surprise when she learned that she would win the reward posted for information leading to the recovery of the boy king. She was even more thrilled, however, to have Coya, through his Indian guardian, bestow upon her the Ivory Charm.

"The trinket belonged to the boy's ancestors. I shouldn't take it," she protested.

"It is a mere trifle to give to one who has saved his life and his throne for him," the man returned gravely.

Although the lad had fully recovered from his recent experience, he seemed older and more dignified than before. He remained at the Drew home for a month, during which time he continued to study English under Professor Stackpole. When it was time for him to leave he made a handsome gift to the scholarly tutor.

Meanwhile Carson Drew, through his friend Mr. George, had kept in touch with foreign authorities and was pleased when word came that the way had been paved for Coya's return to his native land. Iama Togara had fled the country in fear of his life, signing a statement

that the handsome little lad was the real heir to the throne. Yet strangely, when the boy learned that he was to sail for the coronation, he did not seem greatly overjoyed.

"I do not want to leave America and my good friends," he said sadly. His gaze traveled from one to another—Nancy, Mr. Drew, Ned, George and Bess. "If I could take you all with me——"

"I fear that is impossible," Mr. Drew declared.

"Why is it impossible?" interposed the lad's guardian. "At least you and your brave daughter could make the trip across the water. Will you not come as our guests? Without you the coronation will have little meaning to Coya."

"Nancy must decide," Mr. Drew replied.

"She finds enough adventure in this country without sailing across an ocean to encounter one," Ned cut in quickly. He hoped that Nancy would decline the generous invitation, yet he knew what her decision would be.

"I'm sure I'd love India," the girl said.

"But it's so far away," Ned protested.

"Perhaps," Nancy agreed, smiling. "But I would go to the very ends of the earth to find another mystery."

This was not to be necessary for the strange events in connection with *The Whispering Statue,* her next adventure, were to take place not far from the girl's house.

THE END

THE NANCY DREW MYSTERY STORIES

by Carolyn Keene

Here is a thrilling series of mystery stories for girls. Nancy Drew, ingenious, alert, is the daughter of a famous criminal lawyer and she herself is deeply interested in his mystery cases. Her interest involves her often in some very dangerous and exciting situations.

GROSSET & DUNLAP

Publishers   NEW YORK

The Judy Bolton Mystery Stories

By MARGARET SUTTON

You will not want to miss one of these thrilling stories.

THE VANISHING SHADOW—Judy is constantly pursued by a mysterious shadow. Her brother, a timid but lovable boy, turns out to be a real hero in this dramatic, fast moving story.

THE HAUNTED ATTIC—The Boltons move into a large rambling house reputed to be haunted. Even brave Judy is frightened at the strange rappings and the eerie "crying ghost".

THE INVISIBLE CHIMES—A strange girl is sheltered by the Boltons and Judy tracks down many clues before she uncovers her real identity.

SEVEN STRANGE CLUES—Judy works out seven baffling clues to solve the mystery of a school fire and a prize poster contest.

THE GHOST PARADE—Weird happenings at Thousand Island Camp provide mystery, humor and adventure in this thrilling story.

THE YELLOW PHANTOM—With her quick thinking and courage, Judy rescues a lost friend and solves the mystery of "Golden Girl."

THE MYSTIC BALL—Irene, "the engaged girl," is frightened by a crystal gazer but Judy exposes the trickery and saves her friend's romance.

THE VOICE IN THE SUITCASE—A weird cry leads Judy into excitement and danger in a lonely old house.

THE MYSTERIOUS HALF CAT—Judy and her friends become suspicious of a mysterious old beggar and follow him.

THE RIDDLE OF THE DOUBLE RING—Judy's secret engagement plunges her into a riddle for which there seems to be no answer.

THE UNFINISHED HOUSE—Roulsville, "the ghost town," becomes the scene of another exciting haunted house mystery.

THE MIDNIGHT VISITOR—A wrong turn on the road and a midnight visitor are clues to the hidden writing on a will.

GROSSET & DUNLAP : *Publishers* : NEW YORK